CONFESSIONS OF AN *Almost* MOVIE STAR

Mary Kennedy

BERKLEY JAM BOOKS, NEW YORK

THE BERKLEY PUBLISHING GROUP
Published by the Penguin Group
Penguin Group (USA) Inc.
375 Hudson Street, New York, New York 10014, USA
Penguin Group (Canada), 90 Eglinton Avenue East, Suite 700, Toronto, Ontario M4P 2Y3, Canada
(a division of Pearson Penguin Canada Inc.)
Penguin Books Ltd., 80 Strand, London WC2R 0RL, England
Penguin Group Ireland, 25 St. Stephen's Green, Dublin 2, Ireland (a division of Penguin Books Ltd.)
Penguin Group (Australia), 250 Camberwell Road, Camberwell, Victoria 3124, Australia
(a division of Pearson Australia Group Pty. Ltd.)
Penguin Books India Pvt. Ltd., 11 Community Centre, Panchsheel Park, New Delhi—110 017, India
Penguin Group (NZ), Cnr. Airborne and Rosedale Roads, Albany, Auckland 1310, New Zealand
(a division of Pearson New Zealand Ltd.)
Penguin Books (South Africa) (Pty.) Ltd., 24 Sturdee Avenue, Rosebank, Johannesburg 2196,
South Africa

Penguin Books Ltd., Registered Offices: 80 Strand, London WC2R 0RL, England

This book is an original publication of The Berkley Publishing Group.

This is a work of fiction. Names, characters, places, and incidents either are the product of the author's imagination or are used fictitiously, and any resemblance to actual persons, living or dead, business establishments, events, or locales is entirely coincidental.

PRINTING HISTORY
Berkley Jam trade paperback edition / July 2005

Berkley Jam trade paperback ISBN: 0-425-20467-7

This title has been cataloged with the Library of Congress.

PRINTED IN THE UNITED STATES OF AMERICA

10 9 8 7 6 5 4 3 2 1

This book is dedicated to my dear friend
Dalva Hailstone, who has listened to me
for more years than either of us cares to remember!

Acknowledgments

Thanks to my fabulous editor, Cindy Hwang, who was enthusiastic about the project from the beginning, and to her talented assistant, Susan McCarty, for her help and kindness along the way.

Additional thanks to Michelle Grajkowski, agent par excellence, who is hands down the most positive, encouraging person I have ever met.

Hugs and gratitude to Linda O'Brien, aka Kate Collins, a gifted author and devoted friend, for sharing my wacky sense of humor.

Finally, a big thank-you to Alan, my husband and computer guru, who is endlessly patient with his technophobe wife.

Chapter One

⭐

I THINK IT WAS THE WINK THAT DID IT. OR MAYBE I WAS A LOST cause, anyway? Could a wink from Shane Rockett, Hollywood heartthrob, turn me into a quivering, lovesick cow?

You decide.

This is what happened. One minute his eyes held mine, just like an actor in a spy movie, as the camera rolled for the audition tape. He leaned closer and I tried to concentrate on the golden flecks in his tawny dark eyes, the way his dirty blond hair looped invitingly over one eyebrow. Something flickered in those amazing eyes and then grew still again, alert and watchful. We were inches apart. I tried to ignore how good he smelled. I stared at his lips and suddenly thought of long slow kisses that could melt steel.

Get a grip, Jessie.

I clutched the script in my hand, trying to quiet the rain forest of butterflies that had descended uninvited into my stomach. I knew my lines by heart and didn't have to look down at the page. *So it's true what they said about you.* A statement, not a question.

Just as well I had committed it to memory. It was impossible to look away from those eyes. I thought I was immune to Shane's knock-your-socks-off-sexy good looks, but I was wrong.

I took a deep breath and gave my line. Too bad my voice suddenly ratcheted up an entire octave. "So it's true what they said about you."

I had practiced the line over and over with Tracy, my best friend, because she was the one auditioning for the part. I was just along for the ride. We had rehearsed her speech all different ways, emphasizing key words, until we collapsed in giggles.

So it's true what they *said* about you. So it's *true* what they said about you.

It seemed funny at the time, but I wasn't giggling now. The director had surprised me when he plucked me out of the crowd of Fairmont Academy gawkers and asked me to read for him. And that's how I found myself under the lights, script in hand.

With Shane Rockett. Up close and personal, just inches

away from those broad shoulders and famous smile, I felt like the breath was being sucked out of me.

And that's when Shane winked at me. Like we shared a terrific little secret. "And what do they say, darlin'?" He cracked a halfhearted smile, dangerous and sexy, moving in a little closer. Out of the corner of my eye, I saw Alexis Bright, class drama queen, trying to vaporize me with her glare. She was standing off-camera, next to Tracy. Tracy's expression, hurt and betrayed, turned to concrete. They both wanted to be standing where I was, auditioning with *People* magazine's Sexiest Teen Alive.

"Because sometimes people say things . . ." Shane continued, his voice husky, ". . . that aren't exactly true."

Okay, so the dialogue wasn't Dostoevsky, but do you think I cared? My mind was a blank, because Shane was improvising a little, doing a bit of "business" as the actors call it, and was playing with my hair. Just toying with it a little, lifting a lock of my boring-brown tresses and curling it around his finger. And if his hand just happened to graze my shoulder, sending tingles all the way down to my toes, well, it was all part of the scene, right? It wasn't his fault my heart did a little quickstep.

"Cut!" The assistant director's voice washed over the set. "Thanks very much, and let's see the next person up there. C'mon, people. Chop, chop."

I started to turn away, still dazed from Shane's electric

presence, when he gave my shoulder a little squeeze. "Thanks, darlin'. You made me look good." The two deep dimples that appeared in his cheeks were nearly as beguiling as the sudden sparkle in his eyes.

I found my voice. "Anytime." I grinned at him. I couldn't help myself.

I scurried out of the bright lights, as Alexis Bright practically steamrolled over me to grab my place. She stood on the big black X that was taped on the floor, smiling at Shane as if her life depended on it.

And then I saw Tracy waiting for me. She was standing right at the edge of the set, her dark auburn hair tied back, her backpack slung over one shoulder. She had dressed carefully for the audition in her new white American Apparel T-shirt over Gap cargo pants, white Candies slides, and a silver toe ring. Her good-luck outfit, she called it.

I stared at her face, knowing exactly what was wrong and trying to figure out what to say. It was definitely time for some damage control.

"Wow, you should have warned me. That guy gave me goose bumps—" I began, but she cut me off.

"Let's just get out of here, Jess." She hurried ahead of me, her slides clattering like a Clydesdale's hooves over the perfectly waxed parquet floor. She put one hand on the gleaming railing to steady herself and dashed down the broad marble staircase to the ground floor.

Fairmont Academy for Girls used to be someone's estate, and little touches of luxury still remained here and there. The library had rich mahogany paneling, and an honest-to-goodness crystal chandelier hung from the ceiling. As freshmen, Tracy and I were really impressed by the surroundings, but by the time we had our first taste of quadratic equations in trig class, reality set in.

Forget the chandeliers. Forget the palladium windows. This was still high school.

"Tracy, we can't leave now. They may call you back to read again. What's the rush, anyway?" My words fell on deaf ears since Tracy was making tracks, running like a cheetah toward the glass double doors in the front lobby. I was wheezing a little. Either my asthma had kicked in, or standing so close to Shane Rockett had interfered with my ability to breathe.

Shane Rockett. He had certainly interfered with my ability to think. I tried not to remember how that black T-shirt had stretched over his chest, and the way those perfectly faded Diesel jeans had hugged his long, rangy legs. There wasn't really anything going on between us, was there?

"They may call you back up there," I repeated, sprinting to catch up to her.

Tracy turned to glare at me before stepping out into the waning sunlight. "You don't really think I'm still in the running, do you? I don't have a chance in the world. You nailed the part and you know it." Tracy's face was tight, her expression closed, and my heart sank. All my excitement disappeared quick as breath on a windowpane.

"Tracy, you know that's not true. I would never take that part away from you."

Tracy and I have been friends since third grade and nothing, not even Shane Rockett, could come between us. We both came to a stop, hesitating on the broad concrete steps that led down to a winding drive lined with pine trees. The academy was on top of a hill in Bedford, Connecticut, and the driveway curled all the way down to Main Street.

It was a warm, early summer evening, and glowing ribbons of pink and purple and gold were streaming across the sky. Kids were milling around in small groups, giggling and talking. Fearless Productions' decision to use Fairmont Academy as the setting for *Reckless Summer*, their latest teen flick, was the most exciting thing to ever happen in Bedford.

School was officially over for the summer the very next day, but there was a big turnout for the audition. I was surprised, as it seemed obvious to me that the only parts open were for extras. And who wanted to hang around like a potted plant and be called "atmosphere"? I figured the handful of speaking parts would go to kids in the drama club. And Tracy.

She sucked in a huge breath, then let it out slowly as if she were counting to ten or trying to figure out what to say.

"I didn't even know you could act," she said slowly. "All that time you helped me rehearse, I thought you really wanted me to get the part."

"Tracy, what are you talking about? I can't act." I snorted. "I don't know what that was all about in there, but I was acting on sheer instinct. And adrenaline." *And maybe something else*, I thought, but I didn't say it. Like crazy attraction . . .

"I bet the director liked it," she said a little sadly. "Everybody stopped talking when you were up there with Shane. That's how good you were together."

"I didn't notice." That, at least, was true. I didn't notice anything except Shane standing so close to me I could feel his body heat. "I think Shane can make anyone look good."

Tracy shot me a death look. "There wasn't any buzz when I auditioned with him. No magic at all. He could have been reading the phone book, for all the emotion he put into it."

Ouch. I scrambled for something tactful to say. We sat on the concrete steps outside the front portico, and she pulled a diet root beer out of her backpack, offering me a sip. "I thought you did a great job," I said after a minute. "You did it just the way we practiced. And they let you read a little more than I did, so that means they must have liked you."

Tracy steepled her fingers under her chin, a sudden flash of interest in her eyes. "You think?"

"Sure." I stared out at the newly cut lawn. The air smelled fresh and moist and the whole scene was bathed in a tawny glow. One of the cameramen had called it the "golden hour" when the lighting is the most flattering. "What else could it mean?"

"Maybe they let me read a few extra lines because they weren't sure about me, and when you got up there, they knew right away. I never thought you would get up there and blow all the competition away."

"Tracy, maybe you're forgetting that I didn't even want to audition. I came to keep you company. How would I know that they would pick me out of the crowd?"

The whole thing had been a fluke. First the news that Fearless was going to actually shoot a movie at the academy, and then the call for auditions. Naturally everyone in the drama club made a beeline for the casting call, and I tagged along with Tracy. I was sitting there munching a protein bar when a casting director nudged me on the back.

"Hey, honey," she said, in a voice that could open tin cans. "Get on up there and read this." She shoved a part of the script at me. It was just two pages stapled together and I learned that they were called "sides." You don't get the whole script at an audition. Just sides.

So before I knew it, I was ushered to the front of the room and positioned next to Shane Rockett. *The* Shane Rockett. He was huddled deep in conversation with a cameraman in a baseball cap, but he when he turned to me, his face lit up, just like it did in the movies. "Hi there. I'm Shane. You readin' with me?"

"I'm Jessie," I whispered. I wanted to say something else, but couldn't. I wondered why my brain had been sucked out of my head, just as the director called: "Stand by . . ."

"Just relax," Shane said. A cold sweat broke out on my forehead and dampened my palms. I quickly wiped my hand on my jeans, and looked up at Shane expectantly. "Let me lead," he whispered. "Just pretend we're dancing . . ." He looked into my eyes, and the suggestion didn't sound crazy at all. Dancing, that's all we were doing. Dancing.

"And . . . action!" The director's voice sliced across the room. I shook my head, trying to dislodge the memory of Shane Rockett.

The audition had been like a dream sequence, flowing over me like a delicious fantasy and now I was out in the fresh air, back to reality. My focus now was on Tracy. I tucked my hand behind my back and crossed my fingers, hoping the casting gods would smile on her.

"Wow, is he cool, or what!" Three juniors from Fairmont joined us, sitting down on the broad concrete steps. "When do you suppose they'll let us know?" a cute blonde asked us. "I think I'll die if I get that part, I just know I will." She gave me a caramelized smile. "I saw your audition. I think he liked you," she said, giving me an appraising look.

"No, I'm not even in the running." I shook my head, willing them to go away.

Tracy was sitting very still, her hands clasped around her knees, staring blankly at the technicolor sky. I wondered what her chances were. I hadn't been completely honest when I said she had done a great job. Her acting had seemed a little mechanical, almost wooden, and I think she knew it.

There just wasn't any chemistry between Tracy and Shane, even though he was a walking girl magnet. Females seemed to fall like dominoes in his path, judging from the three sitting next to us.

"Jessie Phillips?" A beautiful young woman with a clipboard called my name as she hurried over. She was wearing vintage jeans, all thready at the kneecaps, a tiny silver eyebrow ring, and a black T-shirt that had *Fearless Productions* plastered across the front. "C'mon back tomorrow at three, we need to talk to you."

I shot a look at Tracy and stood up. "What's up?"

"I have some papers for you to look over. And your parents need to sign all these," she said, thrusting a big manila envelope at me. "Consent forms, contract, shooting schedule, costuming appointments." She shot me a quick look. "You're not union, are you?"

"Union?"

"Good, I didn't think so." She looked relieved. "This is an

indie production, but I guess you know that. Independent film, non-union. So you won't be getting union scale, but the salary's not bad."

I had no idea what she was talking about, but I was beginning to think the impossible had happened. If she was offering me a contract and talking about a salary, that could mean only one thing.

"I'm in the movie?" I blurted out. "Is that what you're telling me?" My heart was pounding and weird little prickles were running over my skin.

She looked at me like I was an alien life form. A not-very-bright alien life form.

"That's what I'm telling you, hon. You're Natalie. Congratulations." Someone called her back to the set, and she took off at a gallop, yelling over her shoulder. "Get those forms back to me as soon as you can."

For a moment, there was dead silence. I felt a lurch inside me as if I had just dropped twenty floors.

"Wow," the cute blonde gasped. "You got the part!" She gave me the once-over and shook her Gwen Stefani locks in disbelief. "You're . . . like a movie star! You'll be kissing Shane Rockett and getting paid for it!"

Her friend giggled. "I'd do it for free!" She pouted prettily and scrambled to her feet to nudge me playfully in the ribs. "So how'd you get so lucky?" She peered over my shoulder at the sheaf of papers I was holding. I glanced down. The contract was on top. It certainly looked official.

"I don't know," I admitted. "I can't believe it turned out this way. I wasn't even supposed to audition. I didn't sign up or anything."

I riffled through the papers, my heart skittering in my chest. The shooting schedule, appointments for wardrobe fittings, the names of contact people at the production office. And more of the "sides" for my part.

How could such a thing happen? I was going to be playing opposite Shane Rockett? I felt like I was having an out-of-body experience.

Then I glanced down at Tracy. What would this do to our friendship?

"YOU KNOW IT WASN'T SUPPOSED TO HAPPEN THIS WAY," I SAID half an hour later. "And just because they offered me the part, doesn't mean I have to take it. I can turn it down." Brave words, and I hoped I really meant them. Could I really turn down this once-in-a-lifetime chance? The reality of the situation was beginning to kick in—I was going to be in a movie with Shane Rockett! Part of me wanted to hang out with Tracy and part of me wanted to lock myself in my room and call everyone I knew!

Tracy and I were sitting in my kitchen, sharing a slice of

lemon cheesecake. Two forks and one luscious six-hundred-calorie slice on the plate between us. Tracy had been deathly quiet all the way home, but now she gave me a tremulous smile.

"Don't be silly, Jess," she said quietly. "Of course you're not going to turn it down. I want you to take the part. I've been thinking, maybe in a funny way, it all turned out for the best."

I glanced up in surprise. "You really mean that?" I looked around to see if a Tracy clone had slipped into the kitchen while I wasn't looking. I couldn't believe my luck. Here I was having a major guilt trip over the Shane Rockett audition, and now she was throwing me a lifeline. "You're not just saying it to make me feel better?"

"No, I think sometimes that things just work out the way they're supposed to." She gave me a smile that was a little frayed around the edges and grabbed the last forkful of cheesecake. "You were way better than I was, and anyway, I think I've gone off the idea of acting."

"You have?"

She nodded. "I'd be a nervous wreck trying to remember all my lines, and I think I'd faint if I had to go up there again with Shane." She paused, her blue eyes clear and serious. "No, Jessie, my acting dream is over. I've been doing some serious thinking, and I have a whole different game plan now. Call it Plan B."

"You want to direct?" I was teasing and she knew it. I re-member a joke going around Hollywood that no one was satisfied with just being an actor.

"Don't laugh, but I want to write," she said very seri-ously. "And I want to take pictures . . ."

"I'm not laughing," I reassured her. "But you're certainly full of surprises." Write and take pictures? I wondered where this was going, and remembered that Tracy had interviewed a photojournalist for a career day project during sophomore year. Maybe she had been more serious than I realized.

"You mean you want to write about the movie? Like a celebrity reporter?" I tried to picture Tracy as Leeza Gibbons and couldn't make the image work. She didn't have the flashy highlights, the carefully layered hair, or the toothy grin.

"Not showbiz stuff. I want to do something with more substance to it. I was thinking of being an investigative re-porter. Catching people in their off-screen moments. Kind of a reality thing, but instead of ordinary people, everybody would be movie stars. I could put together a blog."

I raised my eyebrows. "I'm impressed. But are you sure the film company will let you get away with that? They have their own publicity people, you know. I'm not sure they're going to let you run around with a camera snapping candid shots. What if they're unflattering? You'll be like one of those paparazzi."

I'd heard that Fearless Productions liked to throw their

weight around, and that Mr. Clark, our principal, was having second thoughts about letting them invade Fairmont Academy. If they hadn't made a huge contribution to the gymnasium building fund, they would have been shooting their movie down at the local senior citizen center.

"I bet Miss Adams would let me do it for a special project," Tracy said. "She was a journalist before she became an English teacher. I bet I could even get credit for it."

"It's worth a try," I agreed. "You could talk to her tomorrow." I knew Tracy had been aiming for advanced placement in English class, and maybe she was right. Maybe *Reckless Summer* would be her ticket to success.

And mine.

Chapter Two

⭐

MOM'S REACTION LATER THAT EVENING WASN'T WHAT I HAD hoped for, but I knew she would go along with it in the end. She had spent the day scouting antiques at a cutesy little resort town fifty miles away, and was stashing her "finds" in the garage when I met her. Mom runs an antiques business out of a shop attached to the house.

She's supported the two of us for as long as I can remember and we're very tight. Dad's been out of the picture since I was three, and my only clear memory of him is a day we spent together at the Jersey shore one blisteringly hot summer day. We were building sand castles and that's all I remember about him. End of story.

"Hey, Jess," she said, lugging a wicker coffee table out of

the trunk. "You can help me clean this up this weekend and we'll put it in the shop next to that floral sofa—" She stopped, noticing my goofy grin. "Well, somebody looks happy today. What's up?"

I handed her the contract from Fearless, and she scanned it, biting her lip. "A movie? You want to be in a movie?" She looked at me as if I had just said I wanted to fly to Mars.

"It wasn't supposed to turn out this way." I quickly explained about Tracy and the audition. "But now that they've offered me the part, I really want to do it." I paused, wondering when she would say something. "I'll still have plenty of time to help you with the shop," I added. I knew I had to get Mom on my side fast—or my fifteen minutes of fame would be over before they had begun!

We lugged the coffee table into the kitchen and set it down. She popped the tab on a diet cream soda and took a hefty swig before reaching for the Fearless papers. I shuffled from one foot to the other for five solid minutes while she read every single word. Twice.

"I suppose it's all right," she said doubtfully, signing the consent form. "I want to see what you're going to be wearing, though." She gave me one of her "I'm not kidding" looks over the top of her tortoise-shell glasses.

"Sure, no problem." I agreed. "Probably what I wear after school. Jeans and a T-shirt. It's a family movie. PG-13."

"And I want you to call me to pick you up if there's any

shooting at night. I don't want you coming home in the dark, or grabbing a ride with anyone."

"Absolutely," I said. Mom had bought me a cell phone for such emergencies. "I'll check in with you all the time."

"Hmm." She looked unconvinced. "Can parents visit the set?"

She wants to visit the set? Having your mom visit the set would be beyond uncool. So uncool I couldn't even think of a word for it. But it wouldn't be very smart to say that to Mom, would it? I pretended to think for a moment.

"Gee, Mom, I suppose so." Actually I had no idea. Parents were the last thing on my mind when things had been heating up with Shane Rockett at the audition. "I'll find out for sure tomorrow."

"Do that." She tried for a stern look and then her eyes twinkled and she broke into a big grin. "A movie role! Congratulations, baby," she said, wrapping me into a hug.

I hugged her back, grinning. Whatever happened from here on in, I had Mom on my side.

"THE WHOLE THING WAS FIXED, YOU KNOW. IT JUST HAD TO BE!" Alexis Bright's nasal voice drifted over me the next day as Tracy and I edged our way through the Fairmont cafeteria line. The cast list had been posted that morning by Lisa, the production assistant with the eyebrow ring, and everyone had gathered around to have a look. Alexis had scanned the list for her name, quivered in disbelief, and then started at the top again. No luck. She couldn't believe that she hadn't made the cut.

"It's not the end of the world. We can always be extras," Samantha Lawson said perkily. She and Alexis plunked themselves down at one of the long wooden refectory tables that looked like something out of an abbey. I could feel Alexis's eyes boring into me as I cut ahead to the salad bar.

Alexis gave an elaborate sigh. "Extras? You've got to be kidding," she said in scathing tones. "Do you really think I want to be *extra*?" She spat out the word like it was a hairball. "Don't forget, I played Ophelia once."

Samantha's smile never faltered as she bit into her tuna salad on rye. "But that was in the ninth-grade production of *Hamlet*, Ali," she reminded her best friend. "*Reckless Summer* isn't high school. It's the big time." She giggled. "Remember how Hamlet had braces . . ."

Tracy started to laugh, and covered it up with a cough. I managed to keep a straight face and scooped up a tofu Caesar salad, wishing the line would move faster. I hadn't realized how much jealousy and backbiting there was going to be over the cast announcement.

"As far as I'm concerned, it looks like a lot of no-talent people got the parts," Alexis said loudly. Even though our backs were to her as we hurried through the line, she knew we could hear every word she said. "People with no acting training and no ability."

I peeked over my shoulder. She was staring right at me. No one could ever accuse Alexis of being a good sport.

We sidled by with our trays, heading for the patio, when Tracy leaned down close to Alexis. "Well, you know what they say, hon. When you've got it, you've got it!"

"Ooh, good one," I said under my breath as we hurried outside. "She's never going to forgive you."

"So, Jess, what's on the schedule for today?" Tracy and I were settled at a bright blue umbrella table on the flagstone patio behind the academy. Acres of sun-dappled lawn stretched out in front of us, bordered by clusters of flowering pink azaleas and yellow forsythia. Big glazed pots were filled with swaying palms, and the pond had a stone cherub in the middle. It looked like he was feeding some oversized Japanese goldfish called koi, which swam lazily under the surface.

The Fairmont family used to throw big society parties out here on the patio, and if I closed my eyes I could almost hear violin music drifting on the breeze.

"I have to report to the production office at three sharp, the minute school is out. I'll turn in the paperwork and meet with someone from costuming."

"The production office?"

"That's it." I pointed to a set of sleek metal trailers at the edge of the lawn, near the woods. The production company had hauled them in late yesterday afternoon and they were setting them up as offices and dressing areas. They had already installed telephones and fax machines and computers. Crew members in jeans and tank tops hurried by lugging lights and equipment, but there was no sign of Shane Rockett or any of the other principals, as far as I could see.

I had read that the cast and crew was staying at the Bedford Inn, the nicest hotel in town. I wondered if they would make their appearance after school was officially dismissed at three today. Shane Rockett had practically started a stampede of autograph hunters at the audition. Maybe he had decided to lay low until the coast was clear.

In a few hours, all the Fairmont girls would be gone for the summer, and the film company would have the run of the place. I felt a little thrill of excitement remembering that I'd be one of the chosen few—a cast member of *Reckless Summer*. If Tracy felt even a hint of jealousy, she didn't show it.

"How did things go with Miss Adams?" I asked, remembering her plan to talk to her English teacher.

Tracy beamed. "Better than I had hoped. She thought my video diary was a great idea and gave me some tips. And she cleared it with the principal and some community relations woman from Fearless. The movie people want to make a good impression on Fairmont, she told me, in case they want to come back here to film a sequel. So they're willing to bend the rules and let me shoot whatever I want. They have the final approval on all the photographs, though."

"A sequel? Wow, I never thought of that."

"Maybe you'll get the lead," she teased me.

"Yeah, right." I pretended to blow off the idea, but my heart had gone into overdrive. A sequel!

Yesterday I had zero interest in acting, and now I'm wondering how big my part would be in *Reckless Summer II*. I must have caught the "acting bug," as Tracy would say. I glanced down at the "sides" of the script sticking out of my notebook and resisted the urge to read it over one more time.

We finished our salads and agreed to meet back at the production office at three sharp. Tracy had another meeting scheduled with Miss Adams, and I needed to clean out my locker. Then there was the final assembly at two o'clock when Mr. Clark would give us his usual little pep talk about having a "productive summer." The day was winding down slowly to the final, explosive moment when the assembly bell would ring for the last time and school would be officially over for the summer.

I wandered slowly across the lawn, basking in the sunlight, thinking about my part. What sort of character was Natalie? I wondered. The "sides" only covered a few pages. I had no idea what happened in the script before or after the scene I had read with Shane. Was Natalie someone important to him? Was he important to her? I could hardly wait to get my hands on the complete script! Did they get together in the end? Or was I just a passing fling?

"SUCK IT IN," THE WARDROBE MISTRESS SAID CURTLY. "YOU said you were a size six, these jeans are a six. They should fit like a dream."

"This has got to be the smallest size six I've ever seen," I gasped. I held on tight to the waistband and jumped up and down a little.

Nothing happened.

It was like trying to fit an elephant into a Volkswagen. With a shoehorn.

We were standing in the metal trailer marked WARDROBE—FEMALE and I was going through my first wardrobe fitting. The room was buzzing as actresses stood in their underwear, giggling and exchanging gossip, trying on flirty summer dresses and cute capri pants.

I thought I caught a glimpse of Heidi Hopkins, the hottest young starlet in Hollywood, at the front of the trailer. Her wardrobe was being wheeled in on metal racks like you see in department stores, and all her shoes and jewelry were hanging next to her outfits, stashed in clear plastic Baggies. I was dying to wander over and get a good look at her, but first I had to deal with the incredible shrinking jeans.

"This isn't working," I whispered to Tracy, who was sitting cross-legged on the floor, trying out camera angles. I could feel my hands sweating and a damp, clammy feeling was creeping up my chest toward my neck.

"Mmm, what isn't?" she said absently. She took the lens off her new Nikon, held it up to the light to peer suspiciously at it, then shrugged and slapped it back on.

"These jeans!" I hissed. "They don't fit me! They wouldn't fit Malibu Barbie." A drop-dead gorgeous young actress gave me a funny look, and I quickly plastered a fake smile on my face. "Hi there!" I said weakly. She ignored me and pawed through a selection of black slingback heels, size five–six. Even her feet were dainty. I was beginning to feel like Gulliver.

"Of course they don't fit," Tracy said sagely. She had gotten to her feet and was yanking down the waistband of my jeans. They were so tight, I nearly toppled backward. "Ah, just like I thought," she said. "The tag says they're a size *four*."

The wardrobe lady scurried by with a mouthful of pins and I grabbed her elbow. "Oh miss, I mean, ma'am, excuse me, these jeans are the wrong size."

She took the pins out of her mouth and gave me a look like she had just bitten into a lemon. "Yeah?" She had the "I could care less" tone down pat.

"Yes, you see, they're not a six after all. They're a four."

I tried to pull the waistband down to show her, but it was impossible. The heavy denim was slicing into my midriff, nearly cutting off my air supply.

"They're a four, all right," Tracy piped up.

"And who might you be?" She peered at Tracy from over her rimless glasses. "Are you in the cast?"

"No, afraid not. I'm—"

"Then out!" the wardrobe lady said. She certainly hadn't gotten her job because of any personal charm, I decided. "Only cast members are allowed at fittings." She glanced down. "And what are you doing with that camera?"

"I . . . I . . ." Tracy stammered.

"I'll give you three seconds to answer me, and then I'm calling security. We don't want anyone sneaking around taking pictures. Especially when people don't even have their clothes on."

"Now, Maisie," a familiar, sexy voice said, "don't get your panties in a twist. I can vouch for these two ladies."

All three of us turned to see Shane Rockett grinning at us. He looked very cool, dressed all in black. He was holding a cell phone and it looked like he'd put someone on hold to come to Tracy's rescue. Tracy was staring at him like she'd seen a ghost.

"You see, Maisie, this little lady here"—Shane gestured to me—"is Jessie, my co-star . . ." *His co-star?* Shane either hadn't read the script or had just given me a big promotion. I didn't believe a word of it, but I wasn't going to disagree with him.

"And this other lovely lady is her friend Tracy. She's gotten special permission to take pictures of us. There's a memo about it on the cast bulletin board. We're supposed to show her every courtesy. So be nice, won't you, Maisie, pretty please?" He gave that sexy Brad Pitt grin again. Maisie looked like she was ready to swoon.

"Oh!" She flushed bright pink and bit her lip. "Well, in that case, there's no problem. I didn't know they were friends of yours."

Shane chuckled and wrapped his arm around Maisie's waist. "Oh, they're definitely friends, darlin', and might I say that you are lookin' as pretty as a peach today?"

Maisie melted like warm butter at the compliment. "Get on with you," she said, patting her frizzy blond hair. "Go back to your phone call. We have work to do here." She turned to me. "Now then, honey," she said, with a big smile. "How would you like a nice pair of three-hundred-dollar jeans just in from Paris? And this time they'll be the right size!"

Chapter Three

★

"WOW, IT SHOWS WHAT A WORD FROM SHANE ROCKETT WILL do," Tracy muttered a little later. I had finally been fitted with a pair of really cool boot-cut jeans and a long-sleeved boat-neck jersey top. It was robin's-egg blue, a good color with my hair, according to Maisie. Maisie had suddenly become my new best friend, and had promised to pick out all my clothes herself. Shane was obviously a popular guy with the cast and crew.

Tracy had been busy snapping a whole roll of candid shots, mostly of the girls in the trailer mugging for the camera in funny poses and wild hats. It was all in good fun, and even Maisie got in the act, draping a pashmina shawl over one shoulder and vamping it up.

"If it all goes this smoothly, I'll have it made," Tracy said. "I'm off to a good start. There's just one picture left on the roll," she said, reaching into her pocket for more film. "Too bad I didn't get one of Heidi Hopkins."

"Look, there she is," I pointed out. Heidi Hopkins had catapulted to major stardom after winning a Miss Teen USA pageant when she was sixteen. She had done four movies back to back and her perfect heart-shaped face graced the cover of everything from *People* to *Teen Vogue*.

She was walking toward us, doing the catwalk model strut, placing one foot exactly in front of the other, as if she were following a line painted on the floor. She didn't see us, though, because she was studying her script, her forehead creased in a frown. I tried not to notice that she seemed to be moving her lips as she read.

Heidi was tall, impossibly blond, impossibly thin, and her honey-colored hair was wrapped around curlers the size of orange juice cans. And she was popping a big wad of pink bubble gum in her mouth. *Pop. Splat. Pop. Splat.*

Not the most flattering look in the world.

She popped an enormous bubble, letting it slowly collapse in a sticky mass on her face, and that's when I heard the shutter snap.

Tracy had caught her. And then all heck broke loose, as my grandmother used to say. Three things happened simultaneously.

Heidi Hopkins made a noise like a wounded rhino and charged Tracy at lightning speed, her Velcro curlers flying right off her head as she barreled toward us. "Give me that camera!" she screamed.

Tracy glanced up, startled, and tripped over a light cable.

Flip, a three-hundred-pound security guy, grabbed the camera in midair, just before Tracy crashed to the floor.

And then everybody started yelling at once. Flip insisted that he was going to confiscate the camera, while Heidi wailed that she wanted the photo erased then and there. Tracy scrambled to her feet, shouting that she had permission to film from the head of production and from Mr. Clark, the principal. I think she said something else about First Amendment rights, but it was too noisy to be sure.

It was like something out of *The Jerry Springer Show*, and you just knew nothing was going to be resolved. Flip was trying to figure out how to open the back of Tracy's camera to yank out the film, and Tracy was wailing that he was going to break it. Maisie was crawling around on all fours, picking up Heidi's Velcro curlers that had scattered all over the floor. Heidi had both hands on her head, looking like she wanted to pull her honey-colored locks out by the roots.

And that's when help appeared from an unlikely source. None other than that sexy cowboy, Shane Rockett.

"Hey there, hold on, everybody. Hold on, now! We can

figure this out, if we all just take it down a notch." You'd think he'd taken lessons from the horse whisperer, his voice was so calm and soothing.

Amazingly, it worked. In the end, everybody decided to be cool about the whole thing, and it was all thanks to Shane. With his easy smile and lazy Texas drawl, he convinced the security guy that Tracy meant no harm, and had every right to be taking her pictures.

He promised a pouting Heidi Hopkins that the "bubble-gum shot" would be deleted.

He handed Tracy back her camera.

He convinced the gawkers that the show was over and it was time to get back to work.

And then he turned to me and winked, making my heartbeat ratchet up a notch.

"Well, darlin'," he drawled. "Looks like you girls are causin' more trouble than a cattle stampede." He winked to show he really didn't mean it. And then came the zinger. "How's about I take you both to dinner tonight to show there's no hard feelin's?"

Dinner with Shane Rockett? Tracy looked like she was going to faint, and I think I forgot to breathe for a moment. I grabbed Tracy's elbow just in case her knees buckled, and gave Shane my biggest grin. "That would be great, Shane," I warbled. "We'd love to, right, Tracy?"

Tracy gave me a stricken look. "I can't go," she said miserably. "My mom's picking me up to go to my little brother's soccer game. She'll be here any minute." She looked like she wanted to be zapped up to a parallel universe where there were no little brothers and no soccer games.

"Well, no problem, darlin'," Shane said. "We'll do it another time, and that's a promise." He turned his laser-hot eyes on me. "Looks like it'll just be the two of us, Jessie," he said, putting his arm around my shoulders in a friendly, big-brother way. "Think you're up for some genuine Texas barbecue?" Before I could answer, he steered me out of the trailer toward the patio, where the catering service had set up folding tables and a giant steam table.

I was still wearing the to-die-for Paris jeans, but Maisie didn't say a word. Nothing really mattered at the moment, because this was bound to be the most exciting meal of my life. I was having barbecue with Shane Rockett!

I decided this wasn't a good time to tell him I was a vegetarian.

DINNER WITH SHANE WASN'T AS PRIVATE AS I HOPED IT WOULD be, but then what did I expect? He was a movie star! I should have known that I'd have to share him with the world. Or at least the entire cast and crew of *Reckless Summer*.

He insisted on filling my plate for me as we moved through the line, and frowned when I passed up the barbecue in favor of corn on the cob, potato salad, and baked beans. "I love veggies," I told him. "I'll be back for more later."

"I'll hold you to it, darlin'." What I didn't tell him was that I'd be back all right—there was a Black Forest cake on the dessert table that was calling to me!

We sat with other cast members and crew members at a long metal folding table covered with a red-and-white paper tablecloth. Shane seemed to be on friendly terms with everyone, his conversation punctuated by "darlin'," which seemed to be his favorite word.

I knew it was silly, but I felt a happy little *zing* go straight to my heart every time he called me that. As Tracy would say, I was pathetic! I'd have to be careful around Shane, or I'd be acting like one of those lame groupies who tried to sneak onto the set.

"Nice goin' today, Gus," Shane said to a paunchy man in his early fifties. "I saw you practicing wheelies on your hog in the parking lot this morning. Man, what a sight! The gravel was really flying, bud."

Gus Bartley was sitting across from us, tucking into a giant pile of spareribs. He had already laid claim to a hefty piece of apple pie and had stashed it next to his overflowing dinner plate. He was wearing a bright red *Reckless Summer* T-shirt, stretched tight across his ballooning belly.

I thought about asking Maisie for a *Reckless* shirt, and then wondered if it would be a tacky thing to do. If I ever dared to wear it, Tracy would probably never stop teasing me about it.

Gus grinned and gave him a thumbs-up. "Yeah, I'm getting ready for that scene outside the diner. You know, the one where the motorcycle gang gets thrown out of Gino's and takes off up the highway? And there's a big semi heading their way, charging down the wrong side of the road? The timing's kind of tight on that, and I want to make sure I've got it down pat."

"I know the part you mean," Shane said. He leaned forward, eyes sparkling, clearly jazzed. "And then the police cruiser nearly flips on its side trying to avoid the Harley. Right before the Harley goes into a tailspin and wipes out two other cruisers. Man, what a dynamite scene. You know what I thought when I read it?"

"What?"

Shane laughed. "I'm glad you're going to be the one driving the hog and not me. I owe you one."

Gus smiled, looking pleased at the compliment. "No problem. Just doin' my job." He speared a forkful of barbecue. "By the way, thanks for making them buy me a new Harley, Shane. That other one had been kicked around so much, I was afraid the front wheel was going to roll off any second. And then you'd be minus one stuntman."

"Anytime, man," Shane told him. "Glad to do it. You know how nervous the producers get when I try the tricky stuff." I must have looked puzzled because Shane put down his fork to explain. "I did an action flick in Maui last year, and nearly wiped out on a surfboard. So now I'm restricted to car chases, and that's it. Gus does all the heavy-duty stunts, like jumping off bridges and hanging out of planes—"

"And leaps tall buildings at a single bound," a female voice cut in acidly. I looked up and recognized Crystal Hall sitting a few seats away. I wasn't surprised that she would make such a catty comment because the gossip magazines always called her "the Queen of Mean." Was she this way to everyone, or did she just dislike Gus? I found myself hoping I never got on the wrong side of her.

"Now, Crystal—" Shane cut in.

"Oh, we all know Gus," she said, talking right over him. "He's amazing. Nothing short of miraculous." Her voice dripped sarcasm.

"Ouch," Gus said mildly. He didn't seem too offended by her comment, as if he had heard it all before.

Crystal Hall lit up a filtered cigarette and took a long drag before pushing her dinner away. It looked like she hadn't eaten a bite, and she reached for the coffeepot in the middle of the table. She poured herself a large cup of black coffee and sat back with her arms folded in front of her, as if she wanted to separate herself from the rest of the group. Ms. Warmth, she wasn't.

"Don't you like barbecue?" Shane asked, glancing at her plate. I wondered if he was deliberately changing the subject, trying to direct her barbs away from Gus.

"I'd like a nice Caesar salad," she said petulantly. "But I suppose that's too much to ask, isn't it? I'd forgotten we were shooting in the boondocks. Iceberg lettuce and Velveeta cheese are probably considered gourmet fare in this one-horse town." She gave a harsh laugh at her own joke, but everyone else remained silent.

"Hold on there a minute," Shane said, teasingly. "This is gen-u-ine barbecue." He dragged out the word into three syllables, for comic effect, like a cowpoke. "Good stuff, right, folks? Everybody else seems to be enjoying it." He started on his own overflowing plate, as if to demonstrate how good the food really was. I wondered if he was being diplomatic or just sucking up to the older actress. Crystal Hall seemed like someone who could get on your nerves pretty quickly.

"Hummph," Crystal snorted. "Looks like roadkill to me."

I sneaked a peek at the flamboyantly dressed actress, sure I had seen her in a late-night show on the old-movie channel. She had been a big star before my mother's day, and no one knew for sure how old she really was. Everyone knew enough not to ask.

She was wearing so much heavy pancake makeup that I figured she'd need turpentine to remove it. She had pulled her copper-colored hair back in a high ponytail and was wearing gold hoop earrings. Mom would say she was dressed much too young for her age in a skimpy halter top and hot-pink capri pants.

"And you are the sweet young thing?" she said, fixing me with an evil look.

Sweet young thing? I had no idea what she was talking about.

"Now don't give Jessie a hard time," Shane said easily. "This here is Jessie Phillips, from Fairmont Academy. And it's her very first movie."

"How nice for you," Crystal said, dripping venom. "You play the love interest, I suppose?"

"I don't know exactly—" I began, but she cut me off with a withering look.

"Oh, you *can* talk. I wondered about that." She stood up. "Excuse me, everyone. I think I'll look for some granola bars and fruit." She shot a final, scathing look at the steam table. "I wouldn't feed this stuff to my cat."

"Don't mind her," Heidi Hopkins said, slipping into an empty seat beside me. She smiled at me, so I guessed the scene in the wardrobe trailer that afternoon was forgotten. "The old bag likes to make everyone's life miserable. If you just ignore her, she'll find a new victim. She always does."

Heidi began tucking into the barbecue like she hadn't eaten all day. "Have you met Lu Anne Cobb?" she asked, gesturing to a plump girl in a jeans skirt and a T-shirt.

I nodded to her, hoping I could remember everyone's name. The crew members seemed to know each other very well, and I wondered if they had worked on a lot of movies together. I would have to ask Shane after dinner, I decided. Maybe if I knew a little personal history about each of them, I wouldn't feel like such an outsider.

"So I hear your name is Jessie? And this is really your first part? Wow, you really lucked out." Lu Anne giggled and flapped her arms like she was ready to take flight. She had spiky blond hair and was wearing a funky charm bracelet that jangled every time she moved. "Oh, I didn't mean that the way it sounded. Sometimes I put my foot in my mouth. Ask anybody," she said, and giggled again.

"We love you anyway, darlin'," Shane told her, and she blushed. It looked like no one was immune to his charm.

"Are you an actress?" I asked her. She didn't look like any of the Tinseltown beauties sitting at the table. And she didn't seem like a California girl. I placed her accent as being straight out of the Midwest.

"No, I'm a script girl." I must have looked blank, because she went on. "I sit with the director and make notations on the script, you know, blocking, lighting, things like that. And I make sure the continuity's right."

"Continuity?" I was beginning to wish I had a book called *Movie Making for Dummies*. There were so many things I had to learn!

"Sometimes we have to stop shooting right in the middle of a scene. And we pick it up the next day, but it can't look like there's a break in the action. Do you know what I mean?"

"I think so," I said.

"Say an actress is wearing a scarf in a particular scene, and we stop for the day. I have to make sure she's wearing the same scarf the next day when we start shooting again. And I even have to make sure the scarf 's tied the same way. I can't leave it up to the actress or to Maisie, the wardrobe mistress. If it looks different, they won't get blamed, I will. The audience notices stuff like that. You don't dare make a mistake."

"I never thought of that. It sounds like a very responsible job." I caught myself wishing Tracy were with me. She would have been fascinated to hear how the movie business worked and would be busily taking notes.

"Most of the time it is. I started off as a production assistant." Lu Anne looked over her shoulder as if she were afraid of being overheard. "Sy Templeton is a dream to work for, as long as nobody's late or pulls a hissy fit. Just be prepared when you come to the set, and you'll get along fine with him. And whatever you do, don't fluff your lines. Sy hates that."

"I'll remember that." I had no idea what it meant to fluff your lines, but I was going to make darn sure I didn't do it.

"And another part of my job is to make sure the actors read the script exactly the way it's written," she said, raising her eyebrows at Shane. "So make sure you say exactly what's on the page. There are *some* people here who like to improvise." She smiled to show she was ready to forgive him for anything.

Shane gave a little bow. "Guilty as charged. But I can't help it if I like to have fun with the lines, can I?"

"You know how Sy feels about that, Shane," she said. "He wants them read the way they're written."

"I know." He spread his hands in mock apology. "Lu Anne, you are completely right as usual. I don't know what I'd do without you to keep me on track. I'd be writing my own lines, and Sy would be going nuts." He paused and turned to me. "Speaking of lines, we can run some after dinner if you like." Shane was looking at me very intently, and I felt that same little buzz of attraction I had during the audition. "You probably haven't had a chance to look at the complete script, have you?"

I shook my head. "I don't even have a copy of it. All I have are the sides." *The sides.* The pages of the script containing my part. At least I remembered the right word to use. I wanted to fit in as quickly as possible.

"Well, I think you're going to be surprised. They really

punched up your part, you know. It's a lot bigger than what you auditioned for. You really wowed Sy yesterday."

"I did?" I was giddy with happiness, but trying to look cool about the whole thing.

"Oh Shane," Lu Anne said quickly, "I forgot to tell you. Sy wants to see you tonight to work out some blocking. He'd said he'd like to see you right after dinner."

"Sure, I can do that." Shane took a giant swig of iced tea.

Lu Anne caught me watching him. "It's not one of the scenes you're in, Jessie," she said pointedly. Was she afraid I was going to tag along? I saw a tiny smirk play around her mouth, just for a nanosecond, and wondered if I imagined it. Could she be jealous that I was playing opposite Shane? Did she have a major crush on him? The smirk vanished before I could be sure.

Shane grabbed a roll from the bread basket and smeared it with butter. "Jessie, can I take a rain check on running those lines? If Sy wants to see me, it must be important." He was suddenly all business, pushing away his plate and standing up. Everybody seemed to inhale their food, which was fine with me. I was too nervous to eat anyway, and had just picked at my veggies.

"Sure, that's fine. See you tomorrow then."

"I'll go look for Sy right now," Shane said, moving away from the table. "Thanks, Lu Anne." He squeezed my shoulder as he walked behind my chair. "See you on the set," he said in a low voice. Somehow he managed to pack a lot of sultry promise into the words. I had to remind myself that he did it with everybody. Maybe it was all part of being an actor, or maybe Shane just couldn't help being magnetic.

I watched him leave. It had taken every ounce of my self-control not to stare at Shane, tall and gorgeous, swaggering across the lawn in those Diesel jeans that fit him like a second skin. I allowed myself a quick peek and that's all. I mentally shook myself and turned to Heidi Hopkins. "Heidi, can I ask you something?"

"Sure." She delicately blotted her lips with a napkin. Her lipstick was perfect in spite of the fact that she had just scarfed down a huge plate of barbecued chicken, and I felt slightly envious. I made a mental note to ask her for the brand name.

"Shane talked about running lines together. What does that mean?"

She laughed. Her eyes were a startling cornflower blue and she was just as gorgeous as she was on the cover of *YM*. "It means reading your lines to each other. It's a good way to practice before you have to go on the set in front of the director." She seemed to hesitate, and then rushed on. "At least, that's what it usually means."

"Why did you say *usually*?" I raised an eyebrow. Now my curiosity was working overtime.

She shrugged, and then leaned toward me. "I'll tell you a

little secret, Jessie. With Shane, it can mean anything." She paused. "Here's some advice. He's a great guy, but don't take anything he says too seriously. Running lines can mean whatever he wants it to mean. Get the idea?"

I got the idea all right. I was glad he hadn't caught me checking him out. He had probably already figured out that I was developing a major crush on him. No sense in making it worse, I decided.

"Thanks for the tip." We both stood up at the same time, and I suddenly lost all desire for those scrumptious desserts. Maybe it was just as well Shane had been called away to see about the blocking.

I needed to think about what I was getting myself into.

"I CAN'T BELIEVE YOU HAD DINNER WITH HIM!" TRACY SAID later that night. She had stopped by the house to pump me for information. We were making sundaes in the kitchen, spooning hot fudge over mounds of French vanilla Häagen-Dazs. I didn't feel too guilty, because after all, I had passed up that Black Forest cake on the dessert table!

"I can't believe it either," I admitted. "But it wasn't some intimate little dinner for the two of us. There must have been twenty people sitting on a long folding table they'd set up on the patio. It looks like the whole cast and crew eats together every night. They have the whole thing catered." I didn't bother telling her that judging from the main dish, I was the only vegetarian in the bunch.

"That's even better," Tracy said, adding a handful of walnuts to the top of her sundae. Tracy could eat whatever she wanted and never gain an ounce. I longed to have her metabolism. "This way, you got to meet some of the other cast members. Did you get to know any of them? Were they friendly to you?"

"Oh, they were very friendly. And guess who I sat next to?" I paused for effect. "Your new best friend—Heidi Hopkins!"

"Oh no," Tracy groaned. "I hope she didn't tackle you and throw you to the ground. Or toss a cream pie in your face." Tracy scrunched her long legs under her on the kitchen chair.

"Nothing like that. In fact, she was very friendly. She even told me how to make lipstick stay on all through dinner."

"What!" Tracy sat upright, her feet landing with a *thud*. "You talked about girly stuff?"

I nodded. "She said the trick is to first use lip liner over the whole area of your lips, and then add a layer of powder on top of that. And then I think she said you should add more lipstick—"

"Get to the good stuff," Tracy said impatiently. Tracy clearly wasn't into makeup, but she loved gossip. "Did she give you the inside dirt on anyone?"

"She certainly did. She warned me about Shane Rockett." My lips twitched as I waited for Tracy's reaction.

"She did?" Tracy stopped spooning up Häagen-Dazs long enough to give me a look of pure horror. "Does he have some secret past? Is he an ax murderer? Does he get into barroom brawls?"

"Nothing like that. But she made it clear he likes to play girls along."

Tracy snorted. "In other words, he's just a typical guy. I'm surprised she would say something like that, since you're new to the group. They certainly don't say anything personal in front of me. It's going to be like pulling teeth to get any information out of them. How did you get her to open up to you? I could use some pointers."

"I didn't have to. She volunteered it. She danced around it a little, but basically she told me not to believe a word he says."

"Wow. What did you say?"

"Nothing. We had just finished eating, and I said good night and left."

Tracy thought for a moment. "It sounds like you're going to be right in the thick of things," she said slowly. "The next time they invite you for dinner, do you think I can come along?"

"Sure," I said without thinking. I nearly bit my tongue as soon as the words were out. Was Tracy really going to be welcome at the cast and crew dinners every night? She'd have her camera out, and who wanted to be caught with a mouthful of barbecue? I wondered what sort of agreement she had with the production company.

I was Tracy's friend, but I was also a cast member. I'd have to be careful, or I'd end up right in the middle.

"That's great," she said, turning back to her sundae. "Because it seems like I'm going to have to make some connections with the cast, or I'll never get anywhere. And it sounds like you're already tight with them."

"I wouldn't say that," I told her. "Shane invited me to sit with him this time. Who knows what's going to happen tomorrow night?"

Tracy laughed. "Don't sell yourself short. I think you'll be right back at his side."

"Maybe." I thought of Heidi's warning and that little smirk on Lu Anne Cobb's face. "I think I'll have some major competition, though. He's a girl magnet, remember."

"Nothing you can't handle." Tracy grinned and licked the spoon. "Trust me."

Chapter Four

★

"CHECK THE CALL SHEET, EVERYONE! THAT'S WHAT IT'S THERE for!" I recognized the beautiful girl with the clipboard from yesterday—Tracy told me her name was Julie Simon and she was a production assistant. With her long flowing hair and perfect features, she was a dead ringer for Rebecca Romijn. Even though it was barely six A.M. on the *Reckless Summer* set, she was dressed to kill in a pink ribbed Juicy T-shirt and black cigarette pants. Her kitten-heels were sinking into the damp grass behind Fairmont Academy, but she didn't seem to notice because she was too busy reaming out one of the minor characters.

"Under-threes" they called them, because they had less than three lines of dialogue. "Read the call sheet, and then ask me your question," Julie said, in a voice that could cut glass. "Everything you need to know is up there! The names of all the cast members we need today and the scenes they appear in. All you have to do is open your eyes and look."

"Sorry, I didn't see my name up there," the petite actress said, shrugging.

Julie widened her eyes in mock surprise. "You didn't *see* it? Is that what you're telling me? You didn't *see* your name? *Stevie Wonder* could see your name up there . . ."

I glanced at Tracy and stifled a yawn. "Do you think being drop-dead gorgeous is a job requirement in Hollywood? This has got to be more than mere coincidence, right?" I had already decided that Julie must have gotten her job because of her looks; she had all the charm of an angry Rottweiler.

Tracy dropped her canvas tote bag on the floor and reached for a glazed donut and a bottle of water from the breakfast bar. The catering service had set up a long narrow table piled high with apples and pears, orange juice and granola bars, but the Krispy Kremes were disappearing fast. Tracy peered at the donut, like she was trying to calculate the calorie count. "I think they're probably born that way," she said, as a Kate Hudson clone in a tie-dyed top drifted by. "It's not just the actresses, it's everyone on the set. Take a look around. I feel like I'm trapped in an episode of *The OC*. Or maybe a high school version of *The Stepford Wives*."

Tracy was right. Heidi Hopkins was a standout even in this crowd, but there were plenty of wannabes nipping at her pedicured heels. The girls were right out of a Ralph Lauren ad: sophisticated, beautiful, radiating confidence with their streaky blond locks and Southampton tans. Nobody had even the teeniest, tiniest, subatomic bit of body fat anywhere on their toned bodies. I saw Tracy wince and shove the Krispy Kreme donut back in the box.

"Oh, Phillips, there you are!" Julie hurried over to me, her head tilted to one side, as though she were straining to hear something or someone. I hadn't noticed it before, but I saw that she was wearing one of those headsets like Britney wore on her last concert tour. "I told you, I'll have to get back to you on that," she shouted into headset. "Just chill out, will you?"

"Julie," I began, but she held up her hand like a traffic cop.

"Just a minute," she hissed. She fumbled in her pocket and pulled out one of those Tri-Band cell phones. They cost about a zillion dollars and you can use them to call anyone, anywhere in the world. "I have to deal with this idiot first." She punched in some numbers, her forehead creased in concentration. "Hi Mel, it's me, sweetie! Julie Simon from Fearless Productions," she purred, all honeyed sweetness. She clamped the phone to her ear and moved away a few feet, her musical voice drifting over us. I inhaled a bottle of orange juice, shifting from one foot to the other, waiting for Julie to finish the call. "I love you *more*," she finally cooed into the phone. "*Ciao*, baby."

Tracy raised her eyebrows. I knew she was just itching to take a shot of Julie sweet-talking someone on her cell and rolling her eyes, but did she dare? She whipped out her camera and knocked off a few shots of Julie in profile, hands on her hips and a sardonic Elvis curl to her upper lip. It wasn't a flattering shot, but if Tracy was going for the candid look, she nailed it perfectly.

"I think I'm having a nervous breakdown," Julie said, edging back to us. "You wouldn't believe what I have to put up with—"

She stopped to buttonhole a pretty young girl in a tank top heading for the donuts. "Hey, didn't I tell you not to ask Heidi Hopkins for an autograph? I saw you go up to her when she was coming out of Makeup."

The girl stopped, blinked, and gave a tremulous smile. "Gosh, I'm sorry. I thought it would be okay," she said in a soft voice. "She seemed really friendly—"

"You're an extra," Julie said curtly. "Here's the ground rules. You don't think. You don't talk to the stars. You don't ask them for autographs, either, you got that?"

"But it wasn't even for me, it was for my little nephew . . ."

Julie gave a harsh laugh, nearly dislodging her headset. "I don't care if it was for Tiny Tim. You don't speak, okay?

That's why you're called 'atmosphere.' You're paid to stand there like a potted plant. And you don't talk unless we tell you to."

"Geez, I'm sorry," the girl said, backing away hastily. "It won't happen again."

"You bet it won't," Julie said nastily. "Extras," she snorted. "They all think they're gonna be the next Lindsay Lohan." She glanced at me and snapped her fingers as if she suddenly remembered something. "Phillips," she snapped, "make sure you get together with Lu Anne in Continuity . . . they've beefed up Natalie's part. You've got way more lines and we'll increase your salary. I'll have to check with Accounting to get you the exact figure. Check back with me before you go home today."

"I've got more lines?" I said stupidly. *What kind of lines? Lines with Shane?* I felt giddy with happiness at the prospect. Out of the corner of my eye, I saw Tracy zooming in to catch my look of bug-eyed surprise. I was struggling to look cool, but I probably could have passed for an Edvard Munch painting.

Click. Click. Click. Tracy got off a few more shots before I could rearrange my features. I was beginning to see why people got into fistfights with the paparazzi. Tracy was a friend and all, but she seemed to have developed a real knack for taking pictures at exactly the wrong moment! Before

I could ask Julie for more details, she pounced on her next victim. Or rather, victims.

"Hey!" she screamed at a small crowd of extras standing around the fountain. They turned in unison to stare blankly at her, like cows. "Didn't I tell you to spread out? You're all squished together! Spread out! Some people should be standing, some sitting on the railing . . ." She raised her eyes heavenward, as if for guidance. "Honestly, do I have to do *everything* myself?" Julie stomped off, leaving heel marks in the manicured lawn.

"When is your first scene today?" Tracy said, peering at the call sheet. I noticed she kept her camera half-hidden in the palm of her hand, ready for the next big shot. I pushed down the feeling that there was something sneaky, even a little predatory, about the way she was keeping the Nikon out of plain sight. After all, she had permission to take the shots, so why the secrecy?

"Nothing until nine," I said gratefully. "That gives me time to go to Hair and Makeup and Wardrobe. Hair and Makeup are at seven and Wardrobe is at eight." I studied the call sheet and thought for a moment. "Tracy, doesn't it seem really funny that it's going to take two solid hours to get me ready for two minutes on screen?"

"Not if you want to look like these babes, it doesn't," Tracy said. "Heidi Klum said it takes her six hours backstage to get ready for sixty seconds on the runway." She aimed her camera at Julie pushing the extras in place and got off a few shots. "These should be good," she said happily, slipping her camera in her pocket. "Cruella de Vil making life miserable for the extras. It would be nice to have a little montage of them. *Julie Shows Her Claws . . . Julie Has a Hissy Fit . . . Julie Takes a Swipe . . .*"

"Hey, darlin's," a husky voice said behind us. I barely had time to react before a warm arm slipped around my waist and my senses reeled from a burst of lemony aftershave.

Shane Rockett. My heart went *ka-thunk*, like someone had set up a tiny trampoline in my chest.

"What are you Georgia peaches up to today?" It didn't matter that neither one of us had ever lived south of Staten Island; anything female and under fifty was a Georgia peach to Shane.

"We're just checking the call sheet," Tracy piped up. "Jessie wants to see how many scenes she has with you." I threw her a death glare, but she grinned and ignored me, fiddling with the lens on her camera. I was hoping she wasn't going to zoom in for a close-up on Shane.

"Oh, you heard about the script changes," Shane said. "You spoiled my big moment—I was going to surprise you with the good news."

Tracy stared helplessly at him, practically salivating, and I swallowed hard, trying to get my emotions under control.

Shane looked so adorable this morning in a navy J. Crew knit shirt and a pair of faded cargo shorts. His long muscular body was already tanned and the hair on his legs glistened gold in the sun. I had to drag my attention back to what he was saying. If I wasn't careful, I was going to turn into one of those hopeless groupies that Tracy and I made fun of.

"They must have liked Jessie's acting, because they gave her a bigger part," Tracy said. "And more money," she added, ever practical.

Shane gave a slow, sexy smile. "I know she's a talented actress, but maybe they just liked us together on screen," he said, giving my waist a little squeeze. "I think we created some pretty powerful magic up there." He was standing very close to me, even though there was no earthly reason for him to do so, and I could feel the warmth of his thigh pressing against mine. I glanced up at him and he gave me a very hot wink. *Double ka-thunk.*

"What scenes have they added?" I was ashamed at how quavery and pathetic my voice sounded. It was a hopeless cliché, but it was true. Shane literally took my breath away.

"Didn't anybody give you a copy?" He pulled out a sheaf of papers from his back pocket. "Here, take mine, darlin', I can get another one." I recognized the sides from the audition, and was surprised to see that Shane had written all over his with a red marker.

"Oh, I can't take this copy," I said quickly. "It looks like you've made some sort of notes on it." I looked at the scribbled notations, turning the page to the side, trying to figure them out. The little lines and squiggles reminded me of hieroglyphics.

"I learned that in drama school," he said, looking a little sheepish. "No one else on the West Coast does it, but I trained in New York. I got in the habit, and now I can't break it."

"What are all the little vertical lines for?" Tracy said, peering over my shoulder.

"Those are beats. A beat in acting is like a pause. Sometimes the pause sets up the next line. Or sometimes it just completes the thought. The first thing they taught us at the playhouse was how to divide all our dialogue into beats. Silence can be just as important as a line of dialogue, you know. Silence can be very powerful."

Shane was looking right at me as he said it, and I nodded, trying to look dutifully impressed. *Silence can be powerful.* Probably a good lesson for me to learn, since I have an unfortunate tendency toward foot-in-mouth disease.

"The playhouse? You went to Neighborhood Playhouse in Manhattan?" Tracy was drumming her fingers on her empty water bottle, itching for an imaginary pen. She looked like she was dying to write all this down, but I had the feeling Shane would clam up if she reached for a notebook.

Shane nodded. "I spent almost a year there. And then I

took some private acting lessons from a Stanislavski coach in the Village. He really got me to dig deep. I still use a lot of the emotional memory techniques he taught me when I audition in Hollywood. I figure I might as well use every edge I can get. There's a lot of competition out there. Having some training like this puts you ahead of the pack."

Stanislavski? Digging deep? I was seeing another whole side of Shane, and I had to admit it was exciting to know there was a brain behind the movie-star-hottie persona he projected. I remembered seeing a book by Stanislavski on Mom's bookshelf in her office. *An Actor Prepares.* I made a mental note to find it that night and memorize some key ideas. Maybe I could surprise Shane at our next rehearsal!

"I can't imagine you still have to audition for parts," Tracy said. "I thought your agent just made a few calls, and they offered you the lead."

"Are you kidding? No way!" Shane laughed, and pretended to stub his toe in the dirt, cowboy-style. I noticed he was wearing Adidas flip-flops, going for the casual look, or maybe he was already in costume? "Shucks, ma'am, I have to audition just like everyone else. And I get rejected, too, just like everybody else."

I was about to tell him I couldn't imagine anyone rejecting him when Lu Anne saved me from making an absolute lovesick idiot out of myself.

"Shane! I've been looking all over for you!" she said,

barreling down on us. "Sy wants you for blocking on the inside set. They're setting up scene six right now." She glanced at me, taking in my white shorts and layered tank tops. "And you're supposed to be in Wardrobe in three minutes," she said tartly. "Unless you've decided to wear your own clothes for the part."

"Easy, Lu Anne. We were just discussin' acting," Shane told her. "Having a little informal discussion," he said, trying out the famous Rockett grin on her. "You know us actors, once we get started talking, we just can't stop. I think it's in the genes."

"Well, try to control yourself and your genes," Lu Anne said, before flouncing away. "Sy goes ballistic if anyone's late, and you know Sy. You won't like him if he's angry."

"He sounds just like the Incredible Hulk," I murmured.

I immediately regretted my little joke. Lu Anne stopped dead in her tracks to glare at me, and tapped her watch. "Two minutes, and counting," she said, like she was head of flight control for the space shuttle. She waited until I looked appropriately contrite before continuing her march across the lawn.

"Yikes, what is her problem?" Tracy asked. "I thought all you Southern California types were supposed to be laid-back. She's wired like a radio."

"Oh, she's okay," Shane said agreeably. He peeled his arm

from around my waist and my body temperature immediately dropped ten degrees. He handed me the sheaf of papers. "I think Lu Anne's a frustrated actress," he said, lowering his voice. "She comes from a family of actors, and I guess her career never got off the ground. So she went into Production, but in her mind, that's not the same thing as acting. It's like she couldn't make the cut, and she's never gotten over it. She's like this every time we start a new film, but she quiets down after a few days. You'll see."

AN HOUR LATER, I WAS SITTING NEXT TO HEIDI HOPKINS IN Makeup, which is a thrilling experience if you happen to be a complete masochist. To be fair, it's nothing she says or does. It's just that when you're sitting next to the Golden Girl, staring into the same wall-length mirror, it's impossible not to make comparisons. Gorgeous versus not gorgeous. Killer figure versus average bod. Flawless skin verses a sprinkling of freckles with a budding zit or two. You decide.

I was wondering what the makeup director could possibly do to make her even more beautiful. Heidi already had glowing, luminescent skin and just the lightest of California tans. I stared at my reflection, pale and pasty, and vowed to get more sunshine.

"I've got to get some rays," I said a little nervously. "Sitting next to you, I look like I haven't left the house in years." I pinched my cheeks, trying to get a little color into my face. My face was whiter than Wonder Bread.

"You look fine," Heidi said politely. *Fine?* That's what you say when your eighty-five-year-old aunt asks how she looks in her new polyester pantsuit. I stared up at the harsh fluorescent lights beating down from the ceiling, conspiring to enlarge every pore. The makeup mirror was ringed with dazzling baseball-sized lightbulbs, designed to bring out the worst in everyone.

Except Heidi, of course. She glowed under the heavy-duty wattage.

"I'd go easy on the sun if I were you," she said, leaning over to sip her iced tea. "Wrinkles, you know."

"Really?"

Heidi nodded. "I know a girl who's getting an acid peel next week and she's only twenty-five. She's going to have to hide out for at least a month afterward, and tell everyone's she's in Europe. She had to cancel all her modeling jobs because her skin will be bright red and raw, can you imagine? They warned her she's going to look just like a porterhouse steak!" she said, widening those famous eyes.

"Wow, I'll have to remember that," I said, feeling a little queasy. I glanced at her golden skin, as tawny and perfect as a ripe peach. "But you have a nice tan yourself."

Heidi laughed. "Oh, this isn't real. I get it spray-painted on

every ten days in Beverly Hills." She inspected a flawless arm
and pointed out a thin white line around her finger. "Except I
forgot to take my ring off last week. That's why I've got this
little pale band."

"Spray-painted? You mean, like in an auto shop?"

Heidi grinned. "Something like that. You take off all your
clothes and put on these funny-looking glasses and stand in
a little cubicle. There's jets of paint coming at you from all
directions. It costs an arm and a leg, but it's worth it."

"It looks so real."

"It's already starting to fade," Heidi pouted. "I made them
put a clause in my contract that they'd fly me back to Los An-
geles every two weeks to keep up my tan. I certainly wouldn't
trust anyone here to do it right."

"Wise move." *Spray-painted tans.* I suddenly felt very
provincial, living in my little New England town. What else
was going on in the wide world that I didn't know about?

"Looks like you've been rehearsing," she said, pointing to
the sides I was clutching in my lap.

"This is really Shane's script," I explained. "He loaned it
to me a few minutes ago. You see all those little squiggles—"
I began. I leaned over to show her the markings, but she surprised me by laughing and holding up her hand.

"Save your breath. I know the drill. Stanislavski, method
acting, emotional memory . . ." She ticked off the phrases
one by one on her beautifully manicured fingers. "What am

I forgetting—oh, I know, digging deep." She gave a lusty laugh. "Yeah, digging deep. That's Shane all right. Although I think the term 'shoveling deep' would be more like it."

I was stunned. "You know about his method acting?" I suddenly felt betrayed. Here I thought Shane had confided his innermost thoughts to me, as if we were soulmates. And what did she mean by *shoveling deep*? I pushed down the little curl of suspicion that was gnawing away inside me.

"Sweetie," Heidi said, glancing around, "everyone knows about Shane's . . . uh, technique. When he meets someone new, he likes to come on like a great artiste . . . you know."

I frowned, studying the script in my hands. "I'm not sure I do. Why don't you tell me about Shane, the uh . . . artiste?" I managed a tight smile, my heart sinking. Maybe Shane had been stringing me along, and I had been too blind to see it.

"Well, it's like this. Shane figured out that babes go for the sensitive-artist type, so that's what he becomes. He's like a chameleon. He's a hunk, he's a troubled genius, he's a great actor. Do you get it?" She leaned forward, batting her baby blues at me. "He's whatever you want him to be," she added triumphantly.

"I think I get it." My heart plummeted somewhere to the region of my toes.

Heidi curled in her fingertips to inspect her flawless French manicure, and then stifled a delicate yawn. "And another thing . . . he has this amazing way of zeroing in on what you're looking for, and then playing the part to perfection. That's what makes him a very successful star, and also a real heartbreaker. The guy's catnip to chicks, but I'm sure you've already noticed that."

"So none of it's true? He never studied in New York, and never learned method acting?"

"Oh, I think he spent a summer there, but he's making it out to be a lot bigger than it was. He acts like he's better than the rest of us, but let's face it, he made it on his looks, not his talent."

I didn't know what to say. Was Shane "playing me," as Tracy would say? Or was Heidi trying to warn me away from him because of her own agenda? I looked into her electric blue eyes and it was hard to know what to believe. "I heard he did Shakespeare in the Park."

"Shakespeare in the Park? Oh puhleeze." Heidi finished the last of her iced tea with a slurping sound. "Maybe for a couple of weeks. I think he played an extra—you know, third spear from the left? He's no Hamlet, believe me. When I first met him, he was doing a daytime soap called *Passions*."

"*Passions*?"

"And he turned down a role in *The* OC to do this movie. That's what pays the bills in Hollywood, Jessie. Really popular sitcoms and teen flicks. You can make more in one episode of a WB show that you can in six months of doing Shakespeare in some ratty little theater."

Arnie, the makeup wizard, appeared then, with a suitcase-sized kit of bottles and brushes. He probably had enough makeup for the entire cast of *Aïda*, if you didn't bother with the elephants. "Who wants to go first?"

"Do Jessie first," Heidi said, slipping out of her chair. "I want to get another raspberry iced tea."

Arnie stood behind me and rested his hands on my shoulders, staring at my reflection in the mirror. He pulled my hair back in a ponytail and tilted his head to one side, squinting his eyes as he studied my face. "What do we have here," he murmured to himself. "Nice cheekbones, maybe a little contouring on the nose and chin . . . something for the shadows under the eyes . . ."

"Whatever you think, Arnie. Just do whatever you want." The truth is, I didn't care what he did with the makeup. I was still stunned by the conversation with Heidi, and my thoughts were churning. I knew I should be centered and calm for the shoot, but my heart was doing a salsa rhythm in my chest.

"I think you need a light makeup," Arnie said finally. "Something very young, very fresh, very translucent . . . bronze on the cheeks, peachy-brown on the lips." He peered at me closely, and then his expression turned somber. "Although I see that you have some patches of uneven skin tone on your cheeks. But I guess you already know that?"

Uneven skin tone. His voice was appropriately sorrowful, as if I had contracted a life-threatening illness. "Yeah, I guess. I mean, I suppose I haven't thought very much about it."

"Well, don't worry, we can fix that up with a touch of Max Factor tan pancake," he said briskly. He glanced back in the mirror and did a quick assessment. "Maybe a *lot* of pancake. So," he said, glancing down at the script I was holding. "You're playing Shane's girlfriend, right?"

"I play his girlfriend?" I gulped. I was staring straight up at the ceiling because Arnie had started on my eyes, but a little dart of panic arrowed straight to my heart. "I don't know, I mean, I haven't even looked at the script yet." I could have kicked myself for gabbing with Heidi instead of looking over the pages I was clutching in my lap.

He checked his clipboard. "You're Natalie, right? Then you're playing his girlfriend, hon." He finished my eyes, moved in front of me, and started smearing foundation on my face with a little triangular sponge. He worked quickly, making light, sure strokes over my entire face, extending all the way down to my collarbone. He stopped for a minute to look at his work. "You look a little orange under these lights," he admitted, "but don't worry, you won't look that way on camera."

I glanced in the mirror. *A little orange?* I looked like a walking traffic cone!

"I won't worry about it. Um, Arnie, have you read the whole script? I mean, are you sure about the girlfriend bit? Because I thought Heidi played the girlfriend."

Arnie started slapping blush on my cheekbones, making long sweeping strokes that went all the way into the hairline. "Well, Heidi is the one he ends up with," he said firmly. "But you have a very important part in the film, Jessie. You're Natalie. You're the girl he can't forget." He touched his thumb to my chin and gently turned my face toward the mirror. "Look at that face," Arnie whispered. "You're the one that got away, sweetie."

The one that got away? I looked in the mirror and decided Arnie was seriously delusional. A girl with bee-stung lips, Cleopatra eyes, and a look of sheer surprise stared back at me. Malibu Barbie meets Tammy Faye Bakker!

Chapter Five

★

TRACY POUNCED ON ME LIKE A PANTHER THE SECOND I stepped out of the Makeup trailer. "Mmm," she said, camera in hand. "An interesting look, but I'm not sure it's really 'you,' if you know what I mean. The eyes are a little too retro, maybe it's those false eyelashes. You look like Cher doing 'I Got You, Babe.' " She got off a few quick shots of me squinting into the sun. *Click, click, click.* Tracy Hill, Intrepid Girl Reporter, was beginning to get on my nerves.

"Uh, Tracy, could you cool it for a minute? I'm trying to figure something out here." I thumbed frantically through the script. Where was I supposed to be next? And why hadn't I memorized my lines?

"Smile for the camera," she teased. "Okay, pouting is good,

too," she said when I glared at her. "But you really need colla-
gen lips to get the full effect."

"Tracy, cut it out. I have to tell you, this is getting a little
old. You're driving me crazy with that camera in my face all
the time." I could feel my face threatening to slide off in the
bright sunlight, and found myself hoping there would be
plenty of fans on the set. I was sweating as if I had just run
the Boston marathon, and was in no mood to have my picture taken.

"What's getting old?" she said absently. Tracy was looking
through the lens, trying to line up the next shot. No matter
which way I turned, she was right there with the camera in
my face. Give her a Nikon, and all of a sudden she thinks
she's Patrick McMullan.

I swatted at her as if she were an annoying fly. "Honestly,
Tracy, you're starting to bug me!" I could feel a rivulet of
sweat dripping down my nose and when I wiped it away, I
was shocked to see that my hand was orange. My worst fears
had come true—my face really *was* sliding away!

"Oooh, not a good look," Tracy said, snapping away. "I
don't think you're supposed to touch the paint job. Now
you've got a big white streak running down the middle of
your face. Actually, it's sort of interesting," she said peering
through the lens. "Like something out of a primitive tribe
in *National Geographic*—"

"Jessie Phillips?" I recognized the wardrobe lady named Maisie. "We need you in Wardrobe on the double, hon."

"My makeup is running," I wailed. "Maybe I should go back to Arnie . . ."

"No time for that," she said, taking me firmly by the elbow. "Don't worry, they can fix it on the set. They have a makeup assistant there for touch-ups. You'll be fine. Right now, we need to concentrate on getting you dressed."

I was in and out of Wardrobe in record time. Maisie helped me shimmy into a really cool pair of Earl jeans and a gauzy little green-and-white top that had shoulder ties. Very girly. Below the neck, I looked great. Above the neck, I was a walking disaster. "No costume changes today," she said, checking a list. "You just have one scene with Shane, and it's a quickie. The picnic scene."

"The picnic scene?" My brain raced, quivered as if it were going into full arrest, and then skidded to a stop. *Picnic scene, picnic scene.* I shuffled through my memory banks and came up blank. "I don't remember a picnic scene—"

"Oh, it's new. They just wrote it this morning." She watched me flipping through the pages with trembling hands. "Honey, you're wasting your time. It won't be in there. I just told you, it was an add-on."

"Oh." *An add-on.* I relaxed a little, feeling the tightness in my chest start to ease. If I didn't even have the right pages, they couldn't possibly expect me to have my lines memorized. Could they? "Then how do I—"

"Lu Anne in Continuity," she said, ushering me out the door. "She'll have the new sides. I think you've only got a line or two, so don't worry about it." She gestured to a Paris Hilton look-alike who slouched languidly by the trailer door like an anorexic greyhound. "C'mon in, Laurel, I've got your outfit ready."

I wriggled past Laurel, who favored me with a supremely bored look, and took off at a dead run for the production office to find Lu Anne. *Don't worry about it?* Who was Maisie kidding? In a few minutes, I was going to be up on a soundstage with Shane Rockett, cameras rolling, and I didn't have a clue what to say.

Maybe Maisie was right. Maybe I shouldn't worry about it. Maybe the only rational thing to do was skip the panic attack and dive straight into a complete nervous breakdown!

"There you are!" Lu Anne intercepted me as I was running like a quarterback across the north lawn, the damp grass squishing through my open-toed sandals. "We shoot in five minutes. Get over to the outside set, past the tennis courts! On the double!" She started to hurry away as an angry voice boomed out of her headset.

"Wait a minute, Lu Anne," I panted, clutching her arm. "I need a script. Or at least give me my lines."

"What?" She winced and held the headset away from her

head. It seemed to have taken on a life of its own. It was crackling like a Christmas log, and I could hear someone sputtering in rage on the other end. A malevolent male voice, deep and raspy. Maybe the dreaded Sy Templeton?

"My lines!" I shouted desperately. "I need my lines!" I stood in front of her, prepared to tackle her, if necessary. I was dripping with sweat and I could feel my hair clinging to the back of my neck in limp, spaghetti-like strands. I was a vision of loveliness, no doubt about it.

"You actors," Lu Anne muttered. "You're all alike. As if I don't have enough problems, now I've got to worry about your lines. Next thing I know, you'll be asking me about your motivation." She yanked out a single piece of paper from the thick sheaf on her clipboard and shoved it at me. "Here you are. Natalie, act one, scene five. Picnic, exterior."

"It's only one page."

"This is all you need. It's only one line." She stared at me curiously. "What happened to your face? Geez, Arnie must be losing his touch."

I brushed the sweat off my upper lip, remembering too late about Arnie's paint job. Now I probably had a white mustache. "It's a long story," I muttered, teeth gritted. "They told me someone would be available to—"

Lu Anne ignored me and slammed the headset back in place. "Just cool it, will you?" she shouted to the phantom voice. "I told you, I'm on my way!" She sprinted across the lawn without giving me a backward glance. I hesitated, wondering if I had time to zip back into Makeup when I heard someone calling me.

"Jessie? Here you are! I've been wondering what happened to you! I'm Felicity." A beautiful, impossibly thin blond girl hurried over to me. She grabbed me by the elbow, steering me toward a section of lawn that had been roped off and was ringed with klieg lights. This must be the picnic set that Lu Anne had been talking about, I decided.

"I need a few minutes to study my lines," I said, panic rising in me like a bubble.

"Oh, hon, there's no time for that, you'll be fine," she said, patting my arm as if I were a toddler. "You're an under-three, aren't you?"

Under-three. Under-three. Did she really think I was a toddler? No, an under-three was an actor with less than three lines. "Uh, not really. I play Natalie, Shane's . . . girlfriend." I nearly choked on the words. Was I really playing the girlfriend of the sexiest teen on earth?

"Oh, sorry," Felicity said. "You're a principal, then." I remembered someone had told me that a principal had more than three lines. It didn't mean you were a star, or anyone important, just that you weren't an extra, and you weren't an under-three. She quickly ruffled through her script. "I remember now, you only have one line in this scene, but you have lots more later on."

"I do?" I didn't know whether I should feel excited or panicky. I had lines . . . but where were they? At the rate I was going, I was going to have to improvise!

"Um, Jessie, have you been to Hair and Makeup yet?" she stopped dead in her tracks, peering suspiciously at me, and I cringed. "You look a little disheveled. I can tell you right now, Sy won't like this one little bit." She put her hands on her hips and drew her lips into a thin line, probably picturing Sy Templeton in his Incredible Hulk mode.

Darn! I had forgotten to go to Hair, and my makeup was a disaster. It was so hot, I felt like I was going to melt into a little pool of wax on the floor, like that nasty witch in *The Wizard of Oz*. "It's a long story," I said weakly.

"Well, don't worry about it now. We have someone on the set who can work wonders. They can fix anything." She threw me a quick appraising look. "Um . . . almost anything," she backpedaled swiftly. "Let's get up there now. They're doing the blocking for the picnic scene. We're running late, but that's nothing new. We had a minor problem with the mashed potatoes, but I think they fixed it."

"Mashed potatoes?"

"They look just like ice cream on camera, and of course they don't melt in the heat, so they last take after take."

"Really?" Ice cream made out of mashed potatoes. Who knew? The wonders of movie making were starting to amaze me. Maybe I should look into a college that has a film directing program, I decided. With the right connections, I could be the next Penny Marshall!

"They're really cool," she nodded. "You just add food dye for whatever flavor you want—you know, green for pistachio and red for cherry. But the food stylist screwed up this time and they were too runny. They were dripping all over the place when they tried to stuff them in the sugar cones. A big blob fell on Sy's new Gucci loafers and he went ballistic." She gave a little giggle and I found myself smiling at the thought of Sy Templeton having a meltdown. "Your friend Tracy was right there, snapping away the whole time."

She paused to push a blond tendril out of her eyes. She was a dead ringer for Tara Reid. *Is everyone in Hollywood blond, thin, and beautiful?* I wondered. *Maybe they're all clones!*

"Good for her."

"I hope so," Felicity said doubtfully. "I don't think Sy is going to be too pleased when he sees himself caught on camera. I'd sure like to have that snapshot for my album, though."

"I'll see what I can do," I murmured. I wondered if Tracy had any idea how many people she was annoying with her photo diary. Not my problem-o, I decided.

About twenty cast members were scattered around an area ringed with lights, while a man in a baseball cap and Lakers T-shirt shouted orders to some production assistants who were running around like nervous ants.

"Is that Sy?" I whispered.

Felicity nodded. "The great one, himself," she said with a smirk.

I watched as he made a sweeping circle high above the crowd. He was a good-looking guy in his midthirties, perched on something that looked like a cherry picker as he squinted through the viewfinder of a movie camera. He reminded me of a very sleek, very predatory hawk. There were more cameras and lights and equipment scattered all over the grass, and I noticed Lu Anne darting back and forth, handing out pages of the script.

I spotted Heidi Hopkins talking to Shane Rockett, and she was doing the flirty-girl routine—widening her eyes, tossing her hair over her shoulder, and leaning in close. He whispered something in her ear, and she threw her head back and laughed as his arm crept around her waist. They certainly were chummy, I thought. Just friends, or something more? I felt a little wave of jealousy flow over me, and pushed it away. What was there to be jealous about? Two movie stars talking, that's all. Probably about show business. They were major stars, after all, and I was a bit player.

I was pondering what sort of miracle the makeup person could perform when Alexis Bright sidled by.

"Hi, Jessie," she said with a big smile, raking me with her eyes. As always, she went straight for the jugular. "Nice look," she purred. "I didn't know we were doing a horror flick." Nothing subtle about Alexis. She was wearing a pink tank that showed off her toned shoulders, and her legs looked long and tanned in a pair of white cutoffs.

I was trying to think of a quick comeback when Felicity rescued me. "Alexis, I told you before that the extras are supposed to wait over there until we call for you. Now—go!" She gestured to a cluster of picnic tables where hopefuls were sitting talking and sipping sodas in the bright sunlight.

"Well, excu-u-u-se me," Alexis snorted, and did her wobbly supermodel strut back to the tables, one foot in front of the other as if she were prancing down an imaginary catwalk. She had seen Heidi Hopkins doing it and had probably spent hours trying to perfect it. She glanced at me over her shoulder and her look was pure venom. If looks could kill, I would have been a goner at that very moment.

"Wow, Felicity, you certainly put Alexis in her place." I tried not to gloat, but failed miserably.

"Everybody wants to be a star," Felicity said, shaking her head. "These extras are driving me crazy, and Alexis is definitely the worst. Hey, here's Jessie, everyone," she said, pushing me on the set. "She's ready to go."

"But I'm not ready," I squealed. "I mean, really . . . I'm not . . . you see, I . . ."

I have a habit of stammering and speed-talking when I'm nervous. Felicity was studying me as if I were speaking a foreign language, and my brain was going at warp speed. "I need

Hair and Makeup! I need help!" I blurted out, embarrassed. I was ashamed that my voice had risen to a pathetic, high-pitched squeak, like a cartoon character.

"Oh yeah," she said finally, taking in my bedraggled appearance. "Hair and Makeup. I totally forgot. Don't worry, sweetie, we'll make a quick pit stop first. They'll fix you up."

Too late. Shane Rockett had already spotted me and came rushing over, flashing that killer smile. His blond hair glinted in the sunlight, and he was drop-dead gorgeous in genuine U.S. Army fatigues and a black T-shirt. He radiated sex and confidence the way a towering inferno radiates heat.

"Hello, darlin'," he said huskily. "You're lookin' as pretty as a peach today." He let his eyes roam lazily over me, and I felt myself flush with embarrassment. Was everyone around here blind? Or delusional? Or was this just the way people talked in Hollywood?

"Um, thanks, Shane," I murmured. "We're doing a scene together this morning," I said inanely. "The picnic scene. I'm here for the picnic scene." I caught a whiff of his citrusy aftershave as he leaned close, and immediately had difficulty breathing, much less stringing a coherent sentence together.

"I know, and I'm lookin' forward to it, you better believe it. You know, Jessie, I just can't stop thinkin' about you. I even dreamt about you last night. I'll tell you all about it later."

He dreamt about me! He pulled me close, whispering in that raspy drawl, while his right hand massaged my back.

His voice was very low and sexy, full of heat and promise. Standing so close to him threw me into a state of temporary insanity, and for a moment, I forgot that one, I looked like something out of *Dawn of the Dead*, and two, I didn't know my lines.

Somehow, none of it mattered. I just wanted to stand there forever, with his lips touching my ear and his hand moving in little circles up and down my spine. I think I was getting a little delusional myself. *Movie? What movie?*

"Places, everyone!" a young man shouted from a megaphone, inches from my face, and Shane and I jumped apart. "C'mon, boys and girls, chop chop! We want to get this blocking done before lunch."

"But my hair, my makeup," I wailed softly. I turned around but Felicity, who obviously had the attention span of a gnat, was gone. I spotted a bored-looking young woman talking to a cameraman at the edge of the set. She looked to be in her midtwenties, a little chunky and not one of the cookie-cutter blond beauties. She had a hairbrush stuffed in her back jeans pocket, and was wearing a yellow *Fearless* T-shirt, so I assumed she was one of the crew.

"Are you Hair?" I hissed. No response. "Are you Hair?" I hissed, a little louder. It looked like it would take nothing short of a nuclear explosion to get her attention.

She finally glanced over and favored me with a yawn. "Yeah, what do you need?"

I was amazed that she could ask me that with a straight face. *What do you think I need?* "Look at me! I'm a mess! I need help!"

She gave a heavy sigh, heaved herself out of a folding chair, and sauntered over to me with a look of patient suffering on her face. She gave me a quick once-over, sizing me up like a jockey eyeing Smarty Jones. "Wow, what happened to you? Did you forget to go to Hair and Makeup this morning?"

Welcome to Hollywood.

AS IT TURNED OUT, I DIDN'T HAVE TO LOOK TERRIFIC FOR blocking, after all. All I had to do was hit my mark and not fall flat on my face. The "mark," I learned, is an X taped on the ground right where I was supposed to stop, after I sauntered down the length of the buffet table. One of the assistant directors warned us that we always had to be in the right place at the right time for the camera angles to work out right. It took half an hour just to do the blocking and everyone shuffled around the set like cattle, nosing for position as they found their marks.

"Just don't trip on the cables," a cute cameraman named Joel told me. I looked down and saw coils of black electrical cords snaking through the thick grass around my feet. I resolved to watch my step and not totally embarrass myself.

Shane and Heidi were definitely the heavy hitters in this scene, and the lighting director fiddled with a light meter until he got just the right amount of illumination on them. Shane and Heidi seemed to talk to each other nonstop while Hair and Makeup made endless adjustments to the golden couple.

Heidi looked like perfection itself, and Shane could give Brad Pitt a run for his money any day, I decided. I know Shane caught me staring at him once or twice, because he looked over Heidi's shoulder and gave me a broad wink. It was just a playful wink, nothing more, but heat flooded through my veins and set my skin pulsing.

Makeup—in the person of a cute redhead named Shirley—finally took pity on me and gave me a quick touch-up, right on the set. Afterward, she held up a plastic dime-store mirror for me to check out her handiwork. "Is this okay, hon?"

"It's fine. Much better." I smiled gratefully at her. I could never compete with Heidi in the looks department, but at least Shirley had toned down the bright orange hue and I didn't look like a bad embalming job anymore. I was still sweating like a marathon runner, though, and Heidi caught me mopping my upper lip with the edge of a tissue.

"Hey, can we get a fan over here?" Heidi yelled. "It feels like Malaysia, you guys! It's killing me!" Four people snapped to attention, and within seconds a gigantic fan materialized, as powerful as a wind machine, sending a cooling breeze over us. Heidi flashed me a triumphant look and I gave her a thumbs-up. Apparently the *Reckless Summer* crew was determined to keep Heidi happy, and she knew exactly how to get what she wanted.

The power of stardom, I thought wistfully.

I even managed to relax a little, now that I was finally on the set. Lu Anne was right, I decided. I had only one line in this scene, and I had already made up my mind there was no way I would flub it.

"Do you know your line? Because we're getting ready to shoot any second now." Lu Anne suddenly materialized at my elbow like an irritating ghost. I nodded, feeling a stab of panic. *My line, what's my line? This is no time to go blank!* "Say it," she commanded. "Say your line."

"Uh . . . um . . ." So much for not going blank.

"Oh, for heaven's sake. Just a minute, I'll give you your cue!" She ruffled the pages on her clipboard. "Okay, here it is. You're supposed to be looking at the food on the buffet table, and then Shane walks up to you and says, 'See anything you like, darling?'"

She leaned forward and repeated the line. "See anything you like, darling?" She spoke in a flat voice, like an android in a bad science fiction movie. Suddenly, it hit me. I was saved!

My brain kicked in to high gear, as though someone had jump-started it, and I took a deep breath and began. "I see plenty I like, but I guess it's already taken." Scarlett Johansson, eat your heart out. This was my dramatic debut. Not Tolstoy, and maybe not even grammatically correct, but I certainly wasn't going to argue the point with Sy Templeton.

Lu Anne nodded, a hint of a smile softening her plain features. "Not bad," she grudgingly. "Sy will tell you if he wants a different reading on it." *A different reading? How many ways could you say it?* I wondered. Even Julia Roberts couldn't work any magic on that line. Lu Anne tapped me lightly on the arm with her script. "Next time, be prepared. I won't always be around to bail you out."

Finally, the action began. "Picnic scene, take one!" I nearly jumped out of my skin as a production assistant snapped the clapboard right next to my face. I was ready to begin my slow walk down the length of the buffet table, and my insides were racing with excitement. I was so nervous, I was practically hyperventilating. This was my big moment and I knew I better not blow it!

"A-n-n-n-nd . . . action!" Sy Templeton shouted. He was sitting just a few feet off-camera, squinting through a viewfinder, with trusty Lu Anne at his side.

I caught Lu Anne's eye and she motioned me to start walking. I took a few steps and noticed a cameraman moving next to me, gliding along on a little miniature railway track.

For a moment, I was so distracted, I slowed down and came to a complete stop, staring at him.

And that's when the sky fell in and Sy exploded.

"Cut! Cut! Cut!" he shrieked. "You!" he jumped up out of his seat, and pointed at me, the veins bulging in his neck. "Why are you walking in slow motion? If you moved any slower, you'd be dead! And why did you stop? You ruined the take." A sudden hush fell over the group as everyone stared at me. I could just see the feature article in *Variety*: "Girl Ruins Movie, Gives Sy Templeton Heart Attack."

"Back it up, everyone," he shouted to the crew. "We're going to have to start from the top again." He glared over at me. "Lu Anne, do something with her!" Lu Anne didn't have to be asked twice. She nodded and sprang from her chair like a well-trained seal.

Oh, no! my brain screamed back at me. My mouth went dry and killer wasps buzzed in my stomach as Lu Anne hurried over. Just for a nanosecond, I thought I saw a little smile slide over her face, smoothly lethal, the way a snake glides through the water. Was she happy that I had shown myself to be a not-very-intelligent life form? Why would she even care that I screwed up? It would only make her job harder, and it would probably throw Sy Templeton into cardiac arrest.

"I thought I went over everything with you," Lu Anne said with a world-weary sigh. She ran her hand over her eyes as if she had a killer headache. The set was eerily silent and I felt a golf-ball-sized lump start to swell in my throat as I realized I was the center of attention.

I spotted Alexis standing at the edge of the crowd, bright-eyed with excitement, her face a malevolent mask. She was drawn to my disgrace like a shark to blood. She was grinning from ear to ear.

"Yes, you did, Lu Anne, you did," I said hastily. "I'm really sorry. I suppose I just got a little distracted when I saw that guy moving along the track with the camera. I didn't expect him to be there," I said lamely. "He wasn't there during the blocking."

"Of course he wasn't there during the run-through," Lu Anne said with heavy patience. "We weren't filming then. The opening shot is a tracking shot . . . it's just you walking down the length of the buffet table. The camera moves with you."

"Oh." To say that I felt like a total idiot would be the understatement of the year. So much for my brilliant career in filmmaking!

"Sy doesn't like it when we have to stop filming," she said pointedly. *Gee, really?* She cast a worried look over to Sy, who was conferring with the lighting director, another thirty-something guy wearing a baseball cap. "It costs us money every time we stop, and it's a pain in the butt to set up all the equipment again."

"I get it," I said miserably. "Time is money. I'm really sorry."

"Are we ready to run again?" Sy shouted. "Lu Anne, is she absolutely clear on what she has to do?" He stopped pacing the floor long enough to glare at me, his arms folded across his chest. He looked as if he'd like to lob a grenade at me, if only he had one handy.

"She'll be fine," Lu Anne promised. She pinned me with her Gestapo gaze and steered me back to the taped X on the floor. "Jessie, this isn't rocket science. Here's the deal. You start walking at the beginning of the buffet line, and you end right here, get it? Not three feet to the right, not three feet to the left, but right on the X. I know you can do this." She paused. "And don't forget your line. Shane will walk by with Heidi, and he will give you your cue. All you have to do is respond."

"Don't worry, I'll get it right this time," I said meekly.

Before I knew it, Sy called for "Action" once again, and I dutifully walked down the length of the buffet table, my heart beating like a rabbit's. Why was I so nervous? As Lu Anne said, this wasn't rocket science. Out of the corner of my eye, I was watching for my mark, and I made sure not to look at the cameraman in his Thomas the Tank Engine rig, moving along beside me.

One foot in front of the other, look down at the fake food as if it is delicious, remember to look up in surprise, remember to smile, remember your line . . .

I sneaked a quick peek and saw Shane coming toward me from the opposite end of the buffet table. The scene called for Shane and Heidi to be strolling together arm in arm, and when they reached me, Shane was supposed to do a cute little double entendre and ask me if I saw anything I liked. And then I was supposed to give my line. Meaning yes, I saw something I liked (the delicious Shane himself), but it (or rather, *he*) was already taken by Heidi. Easy, right?

Everything was fine until Shane was at my side, his arm wrapped around Heidi's waist. All three of us were standing in the glare of the klieg lights and I heard a soft click as a camera moved into position for a close-up. Shane gave me an endearing, lopsided smile and said in his trademark drawl, "See anything you like, darlin'?"

I glanced up from the buffet table, just the way we practiced, and found myself smiling back at him. And then there was this awful pause. My mind was a total blank! The silence went on forever—or so it seemed—and I heard a nervous cough from a crew member. Shane was still looking at me, his eyes blazing into mine as if he were willing me to come up with the line! He even raised his eyebrows a little as if to say, *C'mon, it's your turn . . .*

I heard a giant whooshing noise, and I thought my heart

was going to jump out of my chest. I couldn't remember my line! Not a single word of it!

I knew I was roadkill.

And then Sy's voice sliced through the fog in my brain. "Cut!" he screamed.

Chapter Six

★

"EVERYBODY MAKES MISTAKES," HEIDI SAID TO ME LATE THAT afternoon. "Honestly, it was no big deal. I'm sorry Sy practically had an aneurysm over it. Try not to take it personally."

We were sipping iced tea from the catering wagon and I was still mulling over my fiasco in the earlier scene. At the rate I was going, Sy would probably write me out of the movie completely! I had finally gotten the line right on the next take, and breathed a sigh of relief. Once burned, twice shy, though, and I wasn't eager to get back up under the klieg lights again.

"Hi there." A cute, preppy guy with sandy brown hair approached us. "How'd it go today?" I smiled at him, and he stuck out his hand, never taking his eyes off Heidi. "Chad Stevens," he said. "I play Brad. You know, the guy in the diner scene who gets into a fight with Gus."

"I'm Jessie Phillips—" I began.

"I know, I saw your name on the call sheet." He was still staring at Heidi, who was inspecting her manicured nails as if she had never seen them before. "How's it going, Heidi? Are you getting into your part?" he asked, just as the silence was getting uncomfortable.

"I guess," she said shortly. She covered a little yawn and stared at the catering staff unloading industrial-sized serving dishes.

"They gave me a bunch of new sides to memorize this morning. Wish I was a quick study, like you." He gave a nervous little laugh.

"I'm sure you'll be fine," she said shortly. Heidi was obviously in sphinx mode and there was no shaking her out of it. *What is her problem?* I wondered.

Chad squinted at the setting sun for a moment and said hesitantly, "It's sort of cool being in a small town, isn't it? So different from L.A. You can actually breathe the air here." He looked so eager and hopeful, my heart went out to him.

"Uh-huh." Heidi still hadn't bothered to make eye contact with him and was fussing with her long blond hair, pulling it back into a beaded scrunchie. "Jessie," she said suddenly, grabbing my elbow, "I just remembered I promised to help you with your costume for tomorrow morning. We better head over to Maisie before she closes up for the day."

I blinked in surprise and shook my head. "My costume? I don't think I have a scene in the morning—"

"Oh, of course you do, Jessie," she cut in smoothly. She gave my elbow a sharp little pinch and I winced. "You must have been looking at the wrong day. There's an early morning scene, and they've picked out something totally wrong for you. C'mon, we better head over there right now!"

"Will I see you at dinner?" Chad asked. "I can save some places for us. We can all sit together." It was obvious the invitation was really meant for Heidi, and I was just an afterthought. He was staring at her the way a hungry dog looks at a Big Mac.

"I don't think so," she said breezily. "We're going to be busy for quite a while. Gotta run," she added, tugging at my arm. I glanced over my shoulder and saw Chad standing staring sadly at us.

"What's all this about?" I said, struggling to keep up with her. She had linked her arm in mine and was pulling me across the lawn at a near-gallop.

"It's Chad," she said, finally coming to a stop outside the costume trailer. She glanced around nervously as if she thought he had pursued us. "That guy's driving me crazy."

"Chad? He seems so nice." I was baffled. "Do you have a . . . history or something? I mean, have you dated him?" He looked like a poster boy for unrequited love, with those big, melting puppydog eyes.

Heidi sighed. "Dated him? Hah!" she snorted. "In his dreams, maybe. He's been trying to date me for months now. We keep running into each other on films. Did you see *Hearts on Fire*? He did all the pyrotechnics for it. He's a genius at that stuff."

"I think I saw the ads for it." *Hearts on Fire* was a cornball epic about a teenage arsonist who joined the fire brigade and set fires in a midwestern town. I remembered that it went straight to video.

"I played the fire chief's daughter in that flick," Heidi continued, "and Chad was always making excuses to be around me, doing geeky technical stuff. Now he trails around after me night and day. No matter how much I blow him off, he never takes the hint. I hate to be rude, but honestly, the guy just won't give up!"

"But what's wrong with him? He's good-looking, polite, friendly . . ."

Heidi grinned. "I'll tell you a little secret, Jessie. I like bad boys. I can't help myself. Chad is too goody-goody for me. It would be like dating a Boy Scout." She sighed. "Give me a bad boy any day."

A bad boy like Shane Rockett? I wondered. I remembered

how the two of them had eye-locked before on the set. In the next scene, the script called for them to do a little lip-locking. How much would be pretend and how much would be for real?

"So what do we do now? We're bound to see him at dinner." We watched as Maisie came out of the trailer and carefully locked it. I smelled the pungent scent of barbecue sauce in the air and saw the catering staff setting out plates and silverware under a canopied tent. Another night of Beef-a-Rama.

"If we go back there, I'll be stuck sitting with him, I just know it!" She frowned biting her lower lip. "Jessie, the last thing I want to do is give him any encouragement. It would be better to avoid him completely. Maybe we could just skip dinner tonight. I've got some diet soda and pretzels in my trailer. You're welcome to join me."

An idea hit me. So bizarre and off the wall, it just might work. "Heidi, how would you like a real home-cooked meal tonight? Veggie lasagna to die for, with a tossed salad and French bread. Peach iced tea with fresh mint from the garden. And for dessert, the best blueberry pie in the world?"

Heidi gave a delicate snort. "Yeah, right. Like that's gonna happen."

"It could happen," I said, grinning. "If you come to my house for dinner. My mom wouldn't mind, I know she'd love to meet you. As long as you're okay with vegetarian food."

"Wow! I'd love it." Her face broke into a wide smile. "Jessie, I've got a confession to make. I've always wanted to be a vegetarian."

Really? I've got a confession to make, too. I've always wanted to be a movie star. But instead I said, "That's so cool! This would be a great night to start." I watched as Heidi spotted Eddie, her limo driver, and waggled her finger to motion him over. A limo? It looked like I was going to travel in style tonight.

A few moments later, I stepped into the cool, dark interior of the limo and sank into the cushiest backseat you could imagine. It was soft and yielding, enveloping me like an amoeba with armrests. Heidi flipped down a mahogany shelf, reached into a tiny fridge, and handed me a diet cola. Miraculously a little plate of corn chips appeared. I leaned back, happily munching, as a Pink song filled the limo.

The extras all turned to stare at the limo as we pulled away from the academy, and Heidi gave a little figure-eight wave with her right hand, like Miss America. You'd think she was practicing for the Academy Awards or marrying Prince William. "Heid-ee! Heid-ee!" the extras chanted, and I heard someone say, "Who's that with her?" I spotted Alexis Bright flitting back and forth along the chow line, like a vampire looking for a place to land.

"This is great." I sighed happily.

Heidi raised a perfectly arched eyebrow at me. "Always

travel by limo, Jessie, never by cab. Cabs are for people who fly coach." She said this as though it was one of the most important pieces of information she had ever heard, something on the level of the melting of the polar ice cap. I nodded, too happy to disagree with her.

Movie stars, limos, and instant fame. I made a note on a mental index card and tucked it away, deep in the recesses of my brain.

I could learn to like this.

HEIDI CHARMED MY MOM SO MUCH, I THOUGHT SHE WOULD TRY to adopt her on the spot. A quick call on my cell had set the wheels in motion. We were five blocks from my house when I thought to call home and warn Mom that I was bringing a last-minute guest for dinner.

"You're bringing her *here*? Right *now*?" I could just picture my mom standing in the middle of the kitchen, lasagna bubbling in the oven, surveying a towering pile of dirty pots and pans in the sink. My mom is an excellent chef, but a sloppy cook. She never measures anything, sips Chardonnay from a margarita glass, and dances around the kitchen to Fleetwood Mac while everything cooks. Music from her generation, she calls it.

"Mom, it's okay. Heidi doesn't care what the house looks like. She's coming for the food. I told her you're Bedford's answer to Nigella Lawson." I winked at Heidi and she nudged me in the ribs. She might be the most famous teen actress in the world, but we were fast becoming girlfriends.

"My mom's the same way," she said, as we pulled up in front of my house. "She cleans the house before the maid shows up."

I noticed Mom had swept her hair back into a French braid and dabbed on some peach lip gloss in honor of Heidi's arrival. "Heidi, I am so glad I'm finally getting a chance to meet you!"

"Thanks, Mrs. Phillips, it was really nice of Jessie to invite me," Heidi said politely. "Something smells delicious," she said, wandering into the kitchen.

"Oh, it's nothing special," Mom said, flushing with pleasure. "Just a little something I whip together once a week." She tucked back a loose strand of hair, and I wondered if she felt a little nervous meeting Heidi. It's funny meeting someone in person when you've seen their picture on the cover of *People* week after week. I remembered how awkward I had felt with Heidi in the makeup room earlier that day. Now everything had changed, and we were practically best buds.

The doorbell chimed just as Mom was slicing up carrot and celery sticks. "Jessie, could you get that while I put out some veggies and dip for us?"

I scooted down the hallway and opened the door to see Tracy. "What's going on? I spotted the limo outside." She giggled. "Is your mom going to a prom?"

"You're not going to believe who's here," I hissed, pulling her inside and shutting the door. The last thing I wanted to do was alert the whole neighborhood that Heidi "The Hottest Star on Two Coasts" Hopkins was visiting us.

"Who?" Tracy was trying to peer past me, toward the louvered doors leading to the kitchen. *Ha-ha-hah!* The famous laugh drifted down the hallway, light and musical, like a wind chime. Tracy stumbled backward in surprise, clapping her hand over her mouth. Then her face lit up like a pinball machine as realization set in. "Ohmygosh! Is that who I think it is?" She lowered her voice to a whisper. "Is it Heidi Hopkins?"

"No, it's King Tut." I glanced nervously over my shoulder. "Yes, you idiot, of course it's Heidi. She's here for Mom's lasagna special. I was just going to call you and see if you'd like to have dinner with us."

"Would I like to? Do birds like to fly?" Tracy jumped straight up and down and then did a little tap dance. "Wow, I can't believe this. I've been trying to catch up with her on the set all day. This is even better. What a chance for a photo op! It's a good thing I brought my camera." She plunked her backpack on the floor and pulled out her trusty Nikon. "I was going to ask you if you wanted to go out for a quick game of tennis, but this is way better. I can get some good candid shots while she's eating. Maybe I can even get some informal shots in the garden."

My heart sank. I knew I had to lay it on the line with Tracy, whether it hurt her feelings or not. "Tracy," I said sternly, "let's get something straight. Heidi is a guest here tonight. She's not here for a photo op."

"Yeah, well, I know that," she began. "I won't try to catch her with a mouth full of food, if that's what you're worried about. All the shots will be tasteful, no pun intended." She grinned at me, as she fiddled with the lens on her camera.

I decided I would have to be blunt, friend or no friend.

"That means no pictures, Tracy," I said firmly. "No candid shots, no posed shots, no pictures at all! She's an invited guest, just like you."

"Oh, it's Tracy. C'mon in, hon," my mom said, opening the door to the kitchen. "You're just in time for some munchies and then lasagna."

Tracy didn't have to be asked twice. "Gee, thanks, Mrs. P.," she said brushing by me. I noticed she slipped her camera in her pocket, and I wondered if she really planned to honor our agreement.

Half an hour later, Mom served dinner on the patio umbrella table. It was a beautiful early-summer night, and the air was heavy with the scent of roses and lavender. Heidi seemed completely relaxed and leaned back in her chair, staring at the garden. Mom was playing a CD she had bought at a street fair in Santa Fe, and the soft strains of an Indian flute drifted on the evening breeze. The musicians were from Ecuador, doing a cover version of the old Simon and Garfunkel tune "Sounds of Silence." That song gets to me every time, it's so plaintive and bittersweet.

"Wow, I can't believe you get to eat like this every night." Heidi gave a contented sigh. "It sure beats the catering service we have on the set." She helped herself to some French bread and Mom poured more iced tea for everyone. "I think I could stay here forever," she added a little wistfully.

"You might find Bedford boring after being in Hollywood, Heidi," Mom said with a gentle smile. "I think a lot of people would envy your life. Spending weeks or months in exciting places, working with some of the most famous people in the world. I can't imagine what your life must be like." Mom sounded a little envious herself, I thought.

"Yeah, well, life in the fast lane isn't all it's cracked up to be, Mrs. Phillips. I don't get home much and I really miss seeing my little brothers and sisters." I was surprised that her voice wobbled when she talked about her family.

"You have brothers and sisters?" Somehow I had never pictured Heidi being part of an Ozzie-and-Harriet-style family. Next she was going to tell me she had a pet hamster named Sam with an exercise wheel.

"I've got two sisters, and two brothers. I really missed a lot of their growing up, because I was on the road so much."

"On the road? Were you a child star, Heidi?" Mom started clearing the plates, getting ready to serve dessert.

"For two solid years, Mrs. Phillips. I got my first break in show business when I joined the road company of *Annie*."

"Gee, that's great. I didn't know you could sing and dance," I said, impressed. I tried to picture Heidi belting out "Tomorrow" with Sandy the dog at her side, and couldn't summon up the image. She seemed too Hollywood-perfect to play a bedraggled orphan.

"I had to learn fast, believe me," Heidi confided. "The whole thing was a fluke. I went into Manhattan because my best friend was auditioning to play one of the orphans. Her mom and my mom are best friends. It was during the summer and we thought we would make a day of it in New York, go to the audition, go to lunch, and hit some of the shops."

"What happened?" Tracy spoke up. So far she had been on her best behavior, and I hoped she wasn't going to ruin everything by asking for a picture.

Heidi took a deep breath and shook her head. "It's like one of those things you read about in movie magazines," she said. "I was sitting there, reading a book, when the director asked me to read for the lead. For the part of Annie."

"Gosh, what did you do?" I was drawn into the story, thinking that it paralleled my experience with *Reckless Summer*. I had never planned on being in the film and had just been along for the ride with Tracy. She was supposed to be the actress, not me, but then it all turned out so differently.

"Well, I explained that I was just there because of my friend—who was looking daggers at me by this time—and he told me to get up there anyway. I was up on stage before I even had time to think about it."

"And you got the part?" I asked.

"Well, first I had to read for him. And then he asked me what key I sang in! I had no idea what he was talking about. They had a little man sitting at a piano, and I asked him what was the easiest key to sing in. He told me the key of A was the easiest for beginners. So I said I sang in A, and they asked what song I wanted to do. I went blank, and the only song I could think of was 'Happy Birthday.' So I mangled my way through 'Happy Birthday,'" she finished with a laugh. "I was terrible. I never would have gotten a spot on *American Idol*."

"That's pretty amazing," Tracy said.

"I thought so too. The next thing I knew, they were asking my mom when I would be available, and if she could travel with me. We were going to be on tour in thirty-seven states and six countries."

"So your mom went with you, I suppose?" my mother asked. "That's quite a commitment."

Just for a second, a frown flitted across Heidi's face, marring her pretty features. "She wanted to, but she couldn't leave my brothers and sisters. So I ended up having a paid companion go on tour with me. I was gone two years, but I came back home whenever I could."

We all were silent for a moment. Heidi had seemed sur-prisingly young and vulnerable when she was telling the story, and I was thinking to myself that her life suddenly didn't seem as glamorous as I had thought. It sounded as though she had been sad and lonely for much of the time. I couldn't imagine being away from home for two years, espe-cially with someone who was paid to be with me. "How old were you?" I asked.

"I had just turned eleven when I was hired. I played in *Annie* for the next two years, until I started getting too tall to play a kid. And then I started getting teen parts. We moved out to California then, and my whole family lives in L.A. now. I see them every chance I get."

"I don't think I've ever seen any pictures of your broth-ers and sisters in fan magazines," Tracy piped up.

"That's because they're very private people," Heidi said quickly. "After all, I'm the one with the career, and I think they should be able to avoid the limelight if they want to. My parents feel very strongly about that."

"Oh, I'm sure they do," Tracy said agreeably. "I would feel exactly the same way." She locked eyes with me and I knew exactly what she was thinking: She would kill to get a photo op with Heidi's whole family!

We sat talking for another half hour and then Heidi looked at her watch. "This has really been wonderful, Mrs. Phillips, but I think I should call it a night."

My mom looked disappointed. "I was just going to make cappuccino," she protested. "I thought I'd light the candles and we could enjoy the garden for a while longer."

Heidi gave her a wistful little smile. "I'd like that, but I have an early call tomorrow. Six o'clock sharp for Hair and Makeup." She pushed back her patio chair and glanced at me. "You have an early call, too, Jessie. You're in the diner scene, and they're shooting it at the crack of dawn. Sy likes that misty, early-morning light."

"Are you sure? The diner scene isn't until halfway through the movie. Why would we be shooting it now?" I had finally wangled a complete script out of Maisie, the wardrobe lady. I knew Lu Anne would never give me one, and I was sick of borrowing sides from the other actors.

"Oh, we always shoot out of sequence, didn't Lu Anne tell you that?"

I immediately went on red alert. "No, she didn't say a word. I figured that as long as I was prepared for the next couple of scenes, I'd be fine."

"That's a dangerous thing to do," Heidi said, looking concerned. "You could be caught off guard and not know your lines and Sy—"

"I know all about Sy," I said wryly, remembering the shoot at the buffet table. "Believe me, I don't like him when he's angry."

Heidi laughed. "The Incredible Hulk. That's right. I forgot

that you know about Sy's temper better than anyone. Just remember that we could be shooting any scene, at any time. You only have the luxury of shooting in sequence when you're doing a big-budget script. I'm surprised at Lu Anne. She should have explained all this to you."

"Well, I'm glad you tipped me off," I said, sounding casual. Note to self: Was Lu Anne deliberately trying to sabotage my performance? It was worth thinking about.

"I've got to work on some dialogue myself," Heidi said, covering a yawn. "I think I'll get together with Shane when I get back to the set and see if he wants to run some lines with me."

Run lines? Shane? My stomach plunged. Hadn't Heidi told me point-blank that running lines with Shane had nothing to do with acting? Had she conveniently forgotten she had shared that little gem of information with me? A curl of jealousy gnawed at my insides, and I willed it to go away. Having a crush on Shane Rockett could lead to major heartbreak, and only an idiot would go that route, right?

"Do you always memorize your lines the night before?" Tracy asked.

"Well, there's usually plenty of time between takes to get them down cold," Heidi explained. "But Shane's got me all uptight about tomorrow," she added. "I suppose I shouldn't pay any attention, but he told me I was going to forget my lines at a key point in the scene. He saw the whole thing in a dream."

"Wow, that is so cool. He dreamt about you." Tracy gushed like a fan and I felt like kicking her under the table. *He dreamt about me, too!* I longed to say.

"He said he dreams about me all the time," Heidi added, arching a perfect eyebrow. "But you know Shane, he always says that to all the girls on the set. He's just a major flirt. That's his standard come-on line. I wonder if anyone is crazy enough to believe him?"

Big laugh all around. *Who would be crazy enough? Moi! I would be crazy enough to believe him!* I sat staring at my dessert, my face flaming with embarrassment. When Shane told me he dreamt about me, my heart had done a little flip-flop of joy. It was humiliating to know that I had been conned by a master.

"It's amazing what girls will believe from a movie star," Tracy said primly. "I'll have to be on my guard in case he pulls that line with me." No longer the gushing fan, she was now an expert on dealing with horny actors.

I walked Heidi to the limo and said good night. She surprised me by giving me a quick hug. "Thanks so much for everything, Jessie. You're so lucky, you know," she murmured. "You've got such a great life." She offered Tracy a ride home and I watched my best friend slide into the backseat with an expression of utter delight on her face. I smiled to myself. Looked like the Hollywood bug had bitten her, too.

Strolling back up the front walk, I let myself think about

Shane. Nothing like a dose of reality to cure the lovesick blues, is there? I felt like I had been hit in the stomach with a sandbag. Busy guy, that Shane. He dreams about Heidi, he dreams about me, he dreams about every available female on the set! I laughed to myself, wondering if he even carried his little black book to bed with him.

Chapter Seven

★

YOU KNOW HOW EVERYTHING IS GOING ALONG SMOOTHLY, AND then *bam*, something hits you out of the blue? I was just drifting off to sleep a few nights later when Mom tapped on my door. "Hon, pick up the phone." She waited and then opened the door a crack. "It's Marc."

Marc! Instantly awake, I shook myself like a wet dog and grabbed the phone. "Hi," I said, my voice coming out in a froglike croak, not the sexy whisper I had planned.

"Hi yourself, sleepyhead. Didn't mean to wake you, but gosh, what are you doing in bed so early?" Marc's voice, warm and husky, raced over the line. I felt my heart do a little quick-step as I scrunched a bed pillow behind my back and tugged the quilt up under my neck.

Marc LaPierre and I met in New Orleans last summer when my mom and I spent time there. His parents own a bed and breakfast called The Black Swan, and we spent an amazing couple of months together. We were both attracted, we were both unattached, but time and distance had separated us. It all seemed like a million years ago. We had exchanged lots of e-mails and IMs and called each other every couple of weeks, but I didn't feel the same dizzying rush of passion for Marc as I was feeling for Shane. Or should I say "felt." Shane was past tense, wasn't he? If only my heart would get the message!

"Jessie, are you there?"

"Sorry, Marc, I was just thinking. I'm in bed because I have an early-morning call tomorrow."

"An early-morning what?"

I had forgotten that Marc didn't know about my part in *Reckless Summer*. I quickly filled him in on everything—the audition, forgetting my lines, trying to fit into those tiny jeans, and Tracy's video diary project. "That about covers it," I finished. *Except for the part about Shane Rockett, I thought. I'm keeping that to myself.*

"Wow, I'm impressed," he said in that sexy, teasing way when I finished my story. "They must have really liked you to give you a speaking part. You'll get to go the wrap party and maybe even fly out to Hollywood for the premiere."

"I guess so. I haven't thought that far ahead."

"Hey, I just thought of something. I can tell everyone I'm dating a movie star!" He seemed ridiculously happy at the prospect.

Dating? If this was dating, it was some new, long-distance version I had never heard of.

"Don't get carried away. I'm not really a movie star. It's only a small part."

"You know what they say." Marc chuckled. " 'There are no small parts, just small actors.' My mom taught me that. She was a theater major at Tulane."

I laughed. "That's a good line. I'll have to remember it." I paused. "So what are you up to?" It was surprising for him to call on a weeknight.

"How'd you like to talk about old times?"

"I thought that's what we were doing right now."

"No, I mean in person. My mom's got some air miles that are going to expire and she's letting me take a round-trip flight anywhere I want. Just for a weekend."

Marc is coming here! "You mean you want to come to Bedford?" I said. It had to be one of the dumbest remarks ever made.

"Gee, that's not much of an invitation," he said, pretending to be hurt. "I thought you'd like to show me around the set."

"Of course I'd like you to come," I said quickly. "I was just surprised, that's all. It would be great to see you. We've got lots of catching up to do."

We talked for another half hour, and Marc filled me in on his parents and what was going on at The Black Swan, their bed and breakfast, and The Gables, the mansion next door. I started to yawn and he laughed. "I think you need your beauty sleep," he said apologetically. "You'll have to excuse me for keeping you up, I've never dated a Hollywood star before."

"Oh, puhleeze! *Reckless Summer* might not win any Academy Awards, believe me. Heidi Hopkins and Shane Rockett are just doing it between other projects." Oops, I hadn't meant to mention Shane's name, but it didn't matter, because it sailed right over Marc's head as he focused on the luscious Heidi.

"Heidi Hopkins?" Marc was clearly impressed. "Wow, I can't believe it. She's in this month's issue of *Maxim*." I remembered seeing the magazine in the Makeup trailer. Heidi was frolicking in the waves somewhere off St. Thomas, wearing a bikini that was so tiny it could have been made out of dental floss.

"And your point is?" I said archly.

"Nothing, I didn't mean that the way it sounded." Marc laughed, but I expected he felt a little embarrassed. The next thing you know, he'd be asking for a celebrity autograph. And I bet it wouldn't be Shane's.

"Uh, Jessie, do you suppose I'll get to meet Heidi when I visit the set?" *Bingo.* He gave a little nervous cough. "And maybe get, you know, an autograph, or a picture or something? If it wouldn't be too much trouble?"

"I'll see what I can do," I said ungraciously. What was it with boys and movie stars? Tracy was right. They were all suckers for gorgeous blondes with legs that went on forever. I lay awake for a long time after we hung up, thinking about Shane and Marc. So different, both attractive in their own way. I was glad that Marc was struggling with blackout dates, and hadn't pinned down which weekend he was using the air miles to come to Bedford. It could be anytime in the next six weeks. That was fine with me. I needed time to figure out my feelings about a certain sexy cowboy who called everyone *darlin'* . . .

"I'M TELLING YOU, THIS DIALOGUE IS JUST WAY TOO LONG, IT just goes on forever." Heidi said petulantly the next morning on the set. "It's not the way I memorized it."

It was barely seven o'clock and the cameramen were standing around drinking coffee out of paper cups, waiting for Sy to make a decision on the next shot, the diner scene. The extras had pounced on the breakfast food like a pack of starving hounds and I saw Julie cutting the Krispy Kremes in half to make them go further. I grabbed a bottle of Aquafina and shifted from one foot to the other. Tracy was off getting some new batteries for her camera, and Shane was nowhere in sight. I decided to keep a low profile until we actually started shooting. I knew I wasn't Sy Templeton's favorite person and I didn't want to draw any attention to myself.

"Did we have a script revision?" Lu Anne said. "I think this is the original version. Or maybe not. We've got another version here with no date on it." She frowned and flipped through the thick sheaf of papers she always carried on her clipboard. She turned to Sy, the ultimate authority. "Sy, do you want to keep the old version of scene six, or the new one?"

Sy looked irritated, waving his hand around his face as if he were batting away an annoying fly. "Lu Anne, we're going to go with whatever Gary wrote. That's what we're paying him for, remember?" He took a gulp of hot coffee and then winced, wiping his hand over his mouth. "I've asked you a thousand times, Lu Anne, can't you get this coffee the right temperature? I'd like to be able to drink it without scalding myself."

Lu Anne rolled her eyes and gingerly took the steaming cup. "Sorry, Sy. I'll put an ice cube in it for you."

"And add plenty of sweetener. It tastes like battery acid mixed with old socks. Okay, now, what were you saying about the script?"

"We were talking about my speech in the diner scene,"

Heidi said, butting into the conversation. She certainly wasn't afraid of Sy Templeton, I thought admiringly. Maybe that was another one of the perks of stardom and golden blond hair. She was looking drop-dead gorgeous, as usual, in a snowy white Ralph Lauren T-shirt with skintight Miss Sixty jeans. "I like the old version better, Sy. It reads better and it makes more sense in terms of my motivation. I don't know why you changed it."

"Which version does Gary want to use?" Sy asked, ignoring Heidi's comment. Gary Chilton was the screenwriter on the project, but he hardly ever appeared on the set. Maisie told me that screenwriters aren't too popular on movie sets. Actors are always afraid the writers might be checking up on them to make sure they're not changing any of the dialogue. And directors worry that the writers might try to tell the actors how to interpret their lines. So the screenwriters end up being invited to "visit" the set once or twice, at the start of filming, and then are never seen again.

"I think he wants the new version," Heidi said. "He said he punched it up a little, just for me."

"That figures," a raspy voice said from behind me. I turned to see Crystal Hall taking a long drag from a cigarette, clutching a cardigan sweater around her bony shoulders. The early-morning light wasn't kind to her complexion and she looked washed out, haggard, in her thin cotton dress.

Puff. Cough. Puff. Cough. She sounded like she was ready

to cough up a lung. "He's a regular Robin Hood, taking some of my lines and giving them to you, sweetie," she said pettishly. "Men do anything for you, don't they, sweetiecakes? Maybe if I went around scantily clad like you, I'd get the same attention." She spat out the last sentence as if she had just swallowed Listerine instead of coffee.

Heidi looked over at me and winked. We both were thinking the same thing: a scantily clad Crystal Hall wasn't going to ring anyone's bell.

"I'll call Gary at his hotel," Lu Anne said decisively. "I know he's in Manhattan making the rounds of the morning talk shows this week. We've got to get this settled one way or another, Sy. Just give me a few minutes, okay?"

Sy nodded to Sandy. "Take ten, everyone," Sandy, the assistant director shouted. "And not a second more."

"There you are, ready to light up my day." Shane Rockett appeared out of nowhere and slid his arm around my waist. "You're looking pretty as a picture, darlin'. How'd you know blue is my favorite color?" Shane had to have some of the corniest lines I've ever heard, but somehow they worked when he said them in that sexy drawl. I felt myself blushing, absurdly grateful that Maisie had selected a sky-blue Juicy top for me that day. Was it really his favorite color? Who knew? Who cared! It was a silly tingle of ego boost, but I loved it. I grinned at him, finding him unbearably cute.

"I took a wild guess," I said, unable to stop my foolish

heart from hammering out a jazz riff in my chest. Shane's slow-as-molasses smile unfolded, warming me all the way to my toes. Broad-shouldered and lean-hipped in tight fitting Diesel jeans, he looked tan and confident all the way down to his perfectly scuffed cowboy boots.

"So what's going on here?" He stared at the cast and crew members milling aimlessly around the grass. "I was calling L.A. on my cell and I missed all the hoopla. Looks like things here are movin' slower than a groundhog in a sandpit."

"You were calling L.A. now?" Crystal said in a loud voice. "It's four in the morning, West Coast time, sweetheart. Who would want to talk to you at that ungodly hour?"

Shane laughed, refusing to take the bait. "Oh, Crystal, I've got friends who like to hear from me whenever the uh . . . inspiration strikes me to call them. Night owls, I guess." His eyes gleamed wickedly, and he winked at me. *I just bet you do,* I thought. Female night owls, no doubt.

"It must be nice to have friends like that," Crystal said sarcastically. It was obvious that she liked Shane but she wasn't falling for his baloney.

"Oh, you can never have too many friends," he said with mock seriousness. He gave me a little squeeze right under my rib cage and I nearly hiccupped. This wasn't the time to tell him I was ticklish. "Uh, Jessie, darlin', I have that book you wanted back in my trailer. Why don't we mosey over there and I'll get it for you. Looks like we're not going to be working for a few minutes."

Book? What book? My mind stalled.

"An Actor Prepares," he said, as if he could read my thoughts. "That's the book that taught me everything I know about acting," he added, looking at me very intently. "I think you could really get some good tips from it. It'll tell you everything you need to know about method acting, and it explains it way better than I can. We can get it now if you want."

I had a number of choices, and they skittered through my brain, rapid-fire style, like a Beyoncé video. I could go with Shane. I could wait right here. Or I could melt into his arms and surrender to wild kisses. Tough decision.

"Time's a wastin'," he said in that Texas twang. He seemed to sense my hesitation and let his hand drift up my back, coming to a stop on the nape of my neck. I had to make up my mind fast, I decided. Another minute, and he'd be doing a full body massage in plain view of everyone! "They're gonna call us back to the set in a few minutes. Sandy will be back on that bullhorn as quick as fleas on a dog."

I laughed at his down-home, country bumpkin metaphor. What was I puzzling over? It was really a no-brainer and I made up my mind in a flash.

I would go with Shane.

Out of the corner of my eye, I saw Heidi shoot me a visual death ray as Shane took my arm and steered me to the far lawn where the actors' trailers were set up. Shane had a big shiny Gulfstream the size of the Hindenburg. He held the door open for me, and I stepped inside to a welcoming blast of cool air.

It looked like it belonged to a rock star, a palace on wheels with high ceilings and sleek furniture. But I barely had a chance to look around, because the minute the metal door snapped closed behind me, Shane made his move.

I was in his arms in two seconds flat. It happened so fast, it was almost subliminal. "Jessie, I've wanted to do this ever since I met you," he said, his voice husky with desire. Not the world's most original line, but I was in no mood to be critical.

All my senses were on red alert, the blood pounding in my brain, as he leaned forward to press his lips against my hair. He literally took my breath away, and I could feel his heart beating through his shirt. We stood like that for a moment, while he ran the tips of his fingers up and down my arm, leaving a trail of goose bumps. My skin tingled and my heart went into overdrive.

Shane Rockett was the most exciting thing that had ever happened to me. His touch was so light, so tantalizing that I nearly fainted with delight. I was in L-O-V-E.

"I really did bring you in here to give you that book," he murmured in my ear. "But somehow being alone with you just does things to me, Jessie." He started to leave a trail of kisses along the side of my jaw, stopping to nibble my ear in a delicious little aside. "You won't hold it against me, will you?" He gave a throaty chuckle. "I wouldn't want you to think I brought you here under false pretenses or anything."

"I won't hold it against you," I said, struggling to get the words out. I was wobbly from the sexy curve of his smile, the husky throb in his voice. It was like every Shane Rockett movie I had ever seen, except now I was up there with him on the big screen. I felt a dizzying rush, like I was riding a roller coaster with my eyes closed.

"I want to spend lots of time with you this summer, dar-lin', but I don't want to rush you, you know? I want to know everything about you." His voice was tender as he pulled me close, so close I could hear his heart beating. "We'll take it slow, and see where this goes."

"I'd like that," I managed to say past a big, gooey lump of tenderness that had lodged in my throat. "I want to know all about you, too." *Funny,* I thought. *Even though I've only known Shane a short time, in some ways, I feel as though I've known him forever.*

Shane chuckled. "Let's get one thing straight right off. I'm not like anything they say in those fan magazines, Jessie."

"No, of course not. I never would have thought that you were."

"I'm glad to hear you say that. Because, Jessie, I want you

to have a good opinion of me. I wouldn't want you to think a word of what they say is true. It's amazin' to me people would spend good money on that rubbish. As if some tabloid reporter would know all about what I do in my spare time, and my likes and dislikes."

"You're right, it's amazing." I shook my head disapprovingly. I had just read in *StarStruck* that Shane liked pizza with pineapple and pepperoni, and hated girls with nose rings. I was tempted to ask him if it was true, but decided this might not be the right time.

He pulled back to look at me, his tawny, dark eyes intense. "I saw a girl reading one of those rags on the set today, and if my mama hadn't raised me to be a gentleman, I swear I would have ripped it to shreds." His voice quivered with indignation. "I don't know where they get that stuff!"

"I don't either, Shane, but it doesn't matter, because no one would believe a word of it," I told him. "How could anyone believe anything bad about you?"

"I'm glad to hear you say, that, darlin', because whoever is writing that stuff has a powerful imagination." He snorted derisively. "This week's issue of *StarGazer* is the worst. If I had done half the things they say I did, I'd be in jail, not on a movie set."

"This week's issue?"

Shane nodded. "The one that came out on Monday. It

has Julia Roberts and Kirsten Dunst on the cover. I just pray that my mama doesn't come across it."

"I hope not," I said, trying to put some moral outrage in my voice. "I don't think she will, you know." Somehow I just couldn't picture Lily Rockett, who lived in Beverly Hills and wore spandex, zipping into a 7-Eleven for a Big Gulp and spotting her son's picture. She had just been in *Hollywood Moms*, a new reality show about teen stars, and the "moms who look young enough to be their dates." Mrs. Rockett had been featured outside Traders, the hottest new club in L.A., wearing a tiny ice-blue Vera Wang slip dress with chandelier earrings. Her blond hair cascaded down her back as she vamped for the camera, nearly toppling off the curb in her platform Jimmy Choos.

She and Shane were arm in arm, and she pouted prettily, pretending to be annoyed at having to wait in line. Shane was staring moodily down Sunset Strip, in his best James Dean pose, as if he hated the trappings of stardom and would rather be out on the range.

"So, Jessie, can I kiss you?" he broke into my thoughts. As always, the perfect gentleman. Can he kiss me? Can a leaf fall from a tree? My heart had not only come alive, it was threatening to burst out of my chest. There was obviously only one answer to his question. Forget about what they said in *The Rules*, this was no time to play hard to get!

"Yes, yes, yes!" I said, sounding like I had just won a washing machine on *The Price Is Right*. I think I stopped breathing the second his lips touched mine. His warm lips, his blazing eyes, his strong embrace, every sensation was burned into my brain like a memory tattoo.

"This is just the beginning, Jessie, just the beginning," he said, pulling back to tuck a lock of hair behind my ear. "I'm going to get to know all about you"—he playfully touched the tip of my nose—"and learn all your secrets. Then I'll tell you all of mine."

"I can hardly wait," I teased him. I snuggled in against him, feeling ridiculously happy. Not only was Shane Rockett the most exciting teen star in the world, but he was a sensitive guy who wanted to get to know me! I could have died happy at that very moment. There was something in his husky voice that stopped my heart, it really did.

I wondered what would come next. More steamy kisses? A delicate fade as Shane and I retreated into the depth of his trailer?

And then reality intruded. Not only intruded but pounded its way into my consciousness. "Shane! We need you on the set right now!" Three hard thumps on the trailer door shattered the perfect fantasy I was enjoying in Shane's arms. If this was a movie, we had suddenly fast-forwarded to the closing credits. Starring Shane Rockett in the lead, and Jessie Phillips as the almost-girlfriend. I prayed there would be a sequel.

"There you are!" Lu Anne said, as Shane reached around me to open the door. It was obvious she was ticked. "I thought you'd only be gone a minute."

"Time flies when you're havin' fun," Shane said wickedly. "I just stopped in to get Jessie my acting book." Like a magician with a rabbit, he pulled a battered paperback out of thin air. "Here it is, darlin'," he said, presenting it to me. "Lu Anne, I'm sure Jessie will let you borrow it when she's finished."

Lu Anne was still standing on the trailer steps glowering at us, and it was obvious she didn't believe a word of it. "Thanks, but I don't have the acting bug. I have enough to do making sure everything's running smoothly on the set," she added self-importantly.

"And we all appreciate it, Lu Anne, we really do," Shane said quickly. "We'd never stick to the schedule and the budget if it weren't for you ridin' herd on us. I was just sayin' that to Sy the other day. I don't know what we'd do if we didn't have you to keep us in line."

I could see Lu Anne softening. "Well, it's nice to know someone around here appreciates me," she said, tugging at the edge of her oversized denim shirt. "We really do need you, Shane. Sy wants to know which version of the diner scene you think is stronger. I can't get Gary on the phone, and I don't think he's going to care either way. After all, he wrote both of them."

"Then let's go, darlin'," Shane said, pushing me out of the trailer ahead of him. "You know what Sy always says, 'time is money.'" He threw his arm over Lu Anne's shoulders as the three of us walked back to the set. "You see, I have learned something from you, Lu Anne. I'm not a lost cause, am I, darlin'?"

"No, I guess not," she said, in a good mood again.

"Back to work, Jessie," he said to me a few minutes later, when we took our places for the diner scene. "We'll get together later," he whispered before Sandy yelled at everyone to stand by.

I smiled back, having come to two important decisions. One: Shane Rockett was easily the best kisser on the planet. And two: nothing in the world would stop me from reading that copy of *StarGazer!*

Chapter Eight

★

TEMPERS FLARED BEFORE THE SECOND TAKE. A DINER SET had been constructed inside the old Fairmont pool house, with red leather booths, a beat-up Formica counter, and an ancient jukebox that belted out every song Johnny Cash had ever recorded.

It was a surprisingly realistic set, with a battered-looking grill, grungy pots and pans, and typed menus covered in clear plastic sheets. The lunch specials were scrawled on a chalkboard—chicken and dumplings, collard greens, and macaroni and cheese. Warm root beer in Mason jars passed for iced tea. I took a sip and nearly gagged. It looked like swamp water, with little circles of green mold floating on the surface.

"Don't drink that, hon, it'll kill ya." Joe, one of the cameramen, stepped out from behind the dolly. "Props serves it that way on purpose. They figure if it's flat and lukewarm nobody in their right mind will drink it. Then they never have to bother refilling the glasses. Easier for them, and we don't get poisoned."

"I get it. Thanks for the tip." I smiled at him, glad I had hidden my bottle of Aquafina behind the booth. My mouth always felt dry and scratchy under the hot lights and I knew it would be hours until we broke for lunch. As long as I kept the water bottle out of sight, no one seemed to care.

Crystal Hall played the part of Reba, the diner owner, who was described as "a blowsy, smart-alecky woman with a heart of gold." Nobody could accuse Sy of typecasting. If Reba had a heart of gold, Crystal had a heart of tin. Crystal complained nonstop, earning murderous looks from the other cast members. She hated everything about the setup, from the drab cotton housedress she was forced to wear to the harsh fluorescent lighting that showed every flaw. She was standing behind the counter with her hands on her hips, looking pale and tired, her mouth drawn in a thin line. Crystal knew she was showing every day of her sixty-plus years and wasn't a bit happy about it.

"Why do I have to wear this stupid cotton vest over my dress?" she said petulantly. "I look like a greeter at one of those discount warehouse stores. 'Hi there, would you like a cart? Don't forget we have a special on paper towels in aisle eleven.'" She raised her skinny arms to the heavens in a theatrical gesture. "I played Lady Macbeth on the London stage, and look at me now!"

"Oh, not again," Heidi snorted in disgust. "She thinks she's an *artiste*," she whispered to me. "We go through this every time. She's never satisfied with her costume, or her hair, or her makeup, or the lighting. Crystal never seems to understand that she's got to look the part. She'd be wearing a little fringed Chanel suit with Manolo Blahniks if Sy let her get away with it."

"Crystal," Sy said patiently, "your costume is appropriate for the part. If you don't like it, you should have taken it up with Maisie. You had your chance earlier this week, when you were getting costume fittings," he added pointedly. "It's a little late in the game to start rethinking your wardrobe. Anyway, it's out of my control. Now, if you don't mind, I've a movie to direct, here." He turned to Lu Anne and adjusted his glasses while they huddled over the shooting script. There was still some question about which version we were using and all of us felt a little uneasy about our lines. In my own obsessive-compulsive way, I had memorized both versions, so I felt pretty secure.

"What do you mean it's out of your control?" Crystal

demanded. "Honestly, Sy, everything is totally in your control. That's why you're sitting in that chair that says *Director* on it. That's why you make the big bucks."

Sy peered at her over the top of his glasses, looking for all the world like a ticked-off owl. "Lu Anne," he said softly, "do something about her." Lu Anne snapped to attention like a loyal basset hound and hurried to the set. She put her arm around Crystal, leading her a few yards away, while she talked to the older woman in a low, intent voice. It seemed like there was a good-cop, bad-cop routine going on here, with Lu Anne always playing the role of the good cop. But could she soothe Crystal's ruffled feathers?

The rest of the cast looked embarrassed at the outburst, taking a few moments to review their lines, mouthing them silently to themselves. I wondered if there was always this much tension on a movie set, or if Crystal's bad mood had infected everyone. Whoever thought movie sets were fun places to be had obviously never visited a Sy Templeton production!

All except Shane, of course. I saw him chewing gum and cracking jokes with one of the cameramen, as if he didn't have a care in the world. Shane was telling a funny story about appearing on Leno, and the camera guy was doubled up laughing. Maybe that acting book was just as amazing as he said it was, I thought. I'd never seen anyone so relaxed in my life.

Heidi saw me staring, and nudged me. "Pretty amazing, isn't it? I'm always a nervous wreck on the set, but he never lets anything get to him," she said in a low voice. "He laughs and kids around with everyone, and once the red light is on, he comes on full power. I don't know how he does it."

I noticed Heidi had written her lines out on a piece of cardboard and had tucked them just out of camera range. "Sometimes I go blank when I'm stressed," she confided. "There's something so distracting when Sy zooms in for a close-up, I feel like he's right in my face. Sometimes I feel my whole role in his films is one big close-up." I could see why Sy concentrated on close-ups of Heidi. Even in the harsh sunlight, her sun-kissed skin looked flawless. "So what did Shane want?" she said, catching me off guard.

"What?"

"Shane," she repeated, giving me an overly bright smile. "I was just wondering what he wanted to give you, or show you, or whatever, in his trailer." Was I imagining it, or was one eyebrow rising in a quirky look of disbelief? A little smile played around her carefully glossed mouth.

"Oh, just a book on acting." I made my voice deliberately casual. "It's over there, with my water bottle. I'll read it later after the shoot."

"*An Actor Prepares*," she said knowingly.

"You can read that from here?" She must have the eyes of a hawk, I decided.

"No, of course not." There was that silvery little laugh again, the one that sounded like a dozen temple bells ringing in tune. "Let's just say that I know Shane. I know all about his style."

There was dead silence while my brain processed this. Heidi was staring at me with those cornflower-blue eyes, the picture of innocence, but I caught myself suddenly wondering if it was all an act. I flashed on a memory of Paris Hilton dressed in denim overalls, chewing on a weed while she pretended to be enjoying life on a farm in one of those television reality shows. Was Heidi play-acting, too? What was she hinting at? I decided to force her hand.

"His style? You must mean his acting style," I said finally. "Well, there's no mystery about that. He says he's pure method. Just like Marlon Brando was."

Her smile widened. "No, that's not what I meant at all, silly. I meant his style with girls. This is Shane's standard first-date present. A copy of *An Actor Prepares*. He must buy them by the truckload. I'm surprised he didn't offer to autograph it for you." Her voice took on a snide tone, and I could feel our blossoming friendship slipping away. Had it ever existed?

"First date!" I was outraged. "Heidi, you know I'm not dating him." A niggling little thought hit me. What did I call those feathery little kisses in the trailer? He had slipped those strong arms around me, and his husky voice had whispered in my ear, as smooth and sweet as warm caramel. If that wasn't a mini-date, what was it? Heidi's suspicions were very close to being on target, but I would never give her the satisfaction of admitting that to her. I could keep a few secrets myself.

"Hmm, maybe he doesn't look at it that way." I felt myself flush as she gave me a tight, knowing smile. "Think of the trailer, Jessie," she said softly. "Didn't that feel just a tiny bit like a first date?"

I was trying to think of a clever retort when Sandy called everyone back to the set. "Just remember what I said," Heidi whispered as she took her position. "Whatever happened in the trailer is Shane's idea of first base. It's up to you if he gets to second . . . or third."

"I'M TOAST!" TRACY SAID WHEN SHE CAUGHT UP WITH ME later that morning. It was lunchtime when she accosted me in the chow line, grabbing me by both arms. "Jessie, it's all over. You won't believe what's happened. Everything's ruined!" Since Tracy has all the makings of a first-rate drama queen, I didn't react right away. I gently disengaged myself and nudged her ahead of me in line. Whatever crisis was brewing could wait until we hit the salad bar, I decided. I had skipped breakfast, and my stomach was performing a little symphony of growls and rumbles. Embarrassed, I clenched my abdominal muscles as hard as I could, practically pushing them through my spine, like I was following a Denise Austin video.

"So Tracy, you're tellin' me you're toast. How's that workin' for you?" I gave a big, toothy crocodile grin, doing my best Dr. Phil imitation. I was disappointed when she didn't even crack a smile.

"Jessie, this is no time for jokes!" she wailed. "My life is falling apart and you're trying to impersonate Dr. Laura." *Dr. Laura?* Ouch. Maybe I really did need to study *An Actor Prepares*, especially the chapter on using voice and dialogue to create a character.

"Sorry," I apologized. "I was just kidding. What happened? I'm sure it's not as bad as you think."

"Someone stole my camera! I left it in my backpack for a few minutes between takes, and now it's gone." *On second thought, it's pretty bad.* "And . . . that's not the worst thing." She leaned in close, her voice wobbly. "My life is in danger. I'm getting death threats."

No way. I must have misunderstood her. "You're getting what?"

"Death threats. Death. Threats." The words poured out of her mouth in a slow hiss, like my mom's espresso machine at the end of the brew cycle. *Death threats? Make that megabad. Even worse than I thought.* A pit formed in my stomach, but I didn't want Tracy to see my reaction, so I acted supercasual.

"Tracy," I said, giving her a little shove ahead of me, "start from the top. And keep your voice down, because I think we've got an audience."

Two extras ahead of us in line had stopped chattering about the latest *Survivor* show and were eavesdropping like crazy. I spotted Heidi Hopkins standing a few feet away, sipping an iced tea but pricking up her ears like a very alert Great Dane. She was pretending not to listen, but when she locked eyes with me, I could see the wheels churning behind those big, innocent baby blues. I raised my eyebrows at her, and she just blinked back in an appealingly ditzy way.

"Look what I found in my mailbox at the production office." Tracy dug in her overflowing backpack, her chin quivering like a landed goldfish. "I went in there to report my camera missing, and I decided to check my mail." Lu Anne had set up a series of mailboxes so she could give acting notes from Sy to the cast and crew. I usually didn't bother reading them, since Sy seemed to only give notes to the principals like Heidi and Shane. Sy seemed happy enough with the rest of us, as long we remembered our lines and didn't trip over the furniture. As Lu Anne always reminded us, this was acting, not brain surgery.

Tracy opened an envelope, pulled out a single sheet of paper, and handed it to me. I unfolded it and gasped. Someone had scrawled: *NO MORE PICTURES. STOP RIGHT NOW. OR ELSE.*

"That's it?" I said, shaking out the envelope as if I expected something else to tumble out. "No more pictures or else? Or else, what?"

"Honestly, Jessie, use your brain," she said in an exasperated tone. She was speaking slowly as if I were a foreign-exchange student and English was my second language.

"I still don't get it. What does it mean?"

"It means . . . or else something terrible will happen. To me." She leaned close, her voice raspy in my ear. "Like somebody'll kill me. That's my guess. Or course, there could be more than one person involved," she added. "It could be a conspiracy. Maybe there are lots of people out to murder me."

"And maybe Elvis is alive, working at a Wendy's in Tupelo, Mississippi." I took a deep breath. "Tracy, you've got to get a grip here. Who in the world would want to kill you? This isn't *The Bourne Supremacy*, you know."

"Who wants to kill me? Whoever wrote this note, that's who," she said tightly. "I would think that's pretty obvious, Sherlock." She rolled her eyes as if marveling at my stupidity.

Death threats, conspiracies, and missing cameras? I knew it couldn't be true, but a creepy little sensation swept over me, and I could feel the hairs on the back of my neck start to tingle. There was always a chance Tracy had just misplaced her camera, but I had a hunch someone really had swiped it. But why?

I looked at the writing. Block letters written with a thick

felt-tip pen on white paper. Even *CSI* would have trouble fig-
uring this one out. "Could it be a practical joke? You know, a
prank?"

"Hah!" she said scornfully. "This is no prank. They stole my
camera, too, remember? This isn't a coincidence, Jessie, and
it's not a game. Whoever wrote that note must have swiped
my camera. I don't know who they are, or what their problem is, but they mean business." She paused, her eyes suspiciously bright as if she were going to burst into tears any
moment. "Jessie, what am I going to do? I didn't think people
minded me taking their pictures. I have permission from the
production company, and from Fairmont, too. Why would
anyone mind? I've gotten some really good shots. People
should be happy I'm doing the video diary."

"Not everybody's happy," I said gently. I was tempted to
tell her that I'd overheard some cast members complaining
about "Little Miss Shutterbug" catching them in "candid moments," but Tracy looked so upset, I swallowed the words.
There would be time to talk it over later, when she was
calmer.

"What am I going to do?" She looked like she was ready
to have a meltdown.

"Let's just have lunch," I suggested. "We can come up with
a list of possible suspects, like they do on detective shows."

"Okay," she said in a little voice. "I guess you're right."

We edged forward in line, shuffling our way past steaming

trays of sausage and peppers, buffalo wings and chipped beef on toast. With any luck, we could hit the organic salad bar before it was ravaged by the horde of extras. I wasn't sure whether the vegetables were really organic, but it was the only thing I would consider eating from the catering table.

"More of the same slop, I see," Crystal Hall said, elbowing an extra aside to join us in line. "Welcome to the soup kitchen. Sy must save a fortune on this discount catering outfit." She peered at the array of hot and cold selections and sniffed disdainfully. "Barbecued pork, canned corn . . . and what's this? Creamed beef? This is outrageous! Even homeless people wouldn't touch this stuff! My chihuahua back in Beverly Hills eats better than this." She snorted and nudged me in the ribs. "You know, Jessie, we should all band together and complain to Lu Anne, not that it would do any good. She never sees Sy for the cheapskate that he is. She worships the ground that man walks on. She's really got him fooled . . ." she added, her voice punctuated by a violent coughing fit.

"You could try the salad bar, Crystal," Heidi said, coming up behind us. She smiled sweetly as two bit players stood back so she could cut ahead of them. "Lars, my nutritionist, says people should have five or six vegetables every day. And the dark-colored vegetables are the best, like eggplant and spinach leaves, if you want to get enough phytochemicals."

"Fito what? Never heard of them. Anyway, I don't feel like

rabbit food," Crystal snapped. "I'm starving!" She wheezed and coughed a little, not bothering to cover her mouth. "Damn! I've left my cigarettes back in my trailer," she said, patting her pockets. "Now what am I going to do?"

"Then this might be a good time to quit," Heidi offered. "You know Sy doesn't like smoking on the set. He says it's not healthy. And a lot of us are allergic to cigarette smoke, so you'd be doing us a favor if you chewed gum instead."

"What Sy doesn't know won't hurt him," Crystal retorted. "And as for the rest of you, well you know what they say. If you can't stand the heat, stay out of the kitchen!" She cackled at her own joke.

Heidi peered at Crystal's leathery skin and smirked. "Well, it's not just Sy. Everyone knows that smoking is murder on your skin, Crystal. It messes up the circulation and causes wrinkles, you know. Especially in women"—she paused delicately—"of a certain age."

"Thanks for the advice, sweetcakes," Crystal muttered. Her voice crackled with sarcasm. "I'll keep it in mind if I ever get to be a certain age." She turned her attention to Tracy. "What's wrong with you, hon?" she said, shooting her a keen look. "I saw you come flying out of the production office this morning looking white as a ghost, like death warmed over."

I shot Tracy a silent plea: *Say nothing.* "Why, not a thing," Tracy said, looking Crystal straight in the eye. "I was running

late, and I didn't want to miss a single minute of Sy's production meeting. Afterward, he took me to the editing room and
let me see yesterday's dailies. That was quite an honor."

My jaw dropped. Lu Anne had already told me Sy was
very protective of the "dailies," the stock of unedited film that
had been shot that day. Only a chosen few were allowed to
view the dailies, and I was amazed that he had welcomed
Tracy. Lu Anne said that actors always complained that the
lighting was unflattering or the camera hadn't caught their
"best" side. So Sy decided to sidestep the problem entirely. He
barred everyone from the editing room except a few key technical people. There was grumbling about it from the principal
actors, but on the set, Sy's word was law.

"Hmmm," Crystal gave her a hard look as if she didn't
believe a word of it. "Sy invited *you* to see the dailies? That's
certainly a first. I'd like to get a look at them myself. Well, if
you've seen them, you can give us the lowdown on yesterday's shoot. How did that party scene turn out? I remember
you stepped on my line, Heidi. I've warned you about that
before." She glared at Heidi, who was picking at her spinach
salad.

We were all sitting together at a long picnic table under a
giant elm, and a cool breeze wafted over us, ruffling the red-
and-white checkered tablecloth. The redwood tables and
shady spots were reserved for cast and crew. I noticed the extras had played musical chairs, scrambling for seats at card

tables set up in a roped-off area on the hot tarmac. There
was a definite class system going on here, like the "above deck"
and "below deck" parties on the *Titanic*. Except there was no
Leonardo DiCaprio to compensate for being stuck at a
cheesy card table in the blazing sunlight. There were definite
advantages to having a speaking part, I realized.

"I stepped on your line? I didn't do it on purpose!" Heidi
protested. "You were dragging out your speech so much, I
nearly fell asleep. I thought you were finished, and that's why
I came in a little early."

"*You* almost fell asleep during my lines?" Crystal hooted.
"Honey, you should have been a hypnotist. You had everyone in a coma with that long monologue in scene three. You
were talking so slowly, you could have been underwater."

"Hello, ladies," Gus Bartley said, tipping his cowboy hat.
He and Shane were balancing overflowing plates of barbecued beef and the smell was overpowering. "Can we join
you?" Like Shane, Gus was dressed like he had just wandered in from the set of *Lonesome Dove*.

"Can we stop you?" Crystal said nastily. "Gus," she demanded, as he swung his legs over the bench, sitting across
from her, "give me a cigarette. I know you smoke real ones,
not those girly-man menthols."

"Honestly, Crystal, can't you ever learn to ask nicely for
something?" Gus flushed, reaching clumsily into his back
left pocket to pull out a crumpled pack of cigarettes. "Keep

it," he said, pushing the pack across the table. "There are only a couple left."

"Thanks," she muttered.

"What's on for this afternoon?" Shane asked, wolfing down a big glop of barbecue spread on a thick slice of Texas toast. "I didn't get a chance to check the call sheet."

"We've got the motorcycle scene coming up," Heidi told him. She smiled at Gus. "This is your chance to shine, Gus. I think your chase scenes are always the best part of the movie."

"Thank you, ma'am. I'll certainly do my best." He made a mock salute and turned to Shane. "I think we've got some good people riding with us for a change. Three or four of those extras have some stunt experience, so we didn't need to ask for more professionals. And we can use the crew to fill in here and there."

"That's good," Shane agreed. "I can remember when you were the only one who could do the tricky parts, and we had to shoot the same scene over and over, with you wearing different disguises."

"I remember those days too," Gus said ruefully. "One time I hurt my back so bad, I was out of work for six months. It was hard to pay the bills, believe me."

"Yeah, right," Crystal said sarcastically. "I bet you found a way to get some ready cash, though, didn't you?"

There was a long pause, while we all sat in embarrassed silence. I wondered why Crystal seemed to have it in for Gus.

In a carefully choreographed scene, the cyclists would surround Shane and he would chase them at high speed down the highway, with a helicopter buzzing overhead. A posse of black-and-white police cars would join in, with mock crashes and explosions. The "highway" was actually the long, winding driveway to Fairmont Academy, but with the right camera angles, it would pass for a major thoroughfare.

It was one of those car chases that you see in every action-adventure movie, and I bet it would keep everyone on the edge of their seats. I had heard some of the crew members planning it and talking about the risks involved. I had double-checked the call sheet, relieved that I wasn't listed for the scene.

"Why wouldn't you want to use professionals?" Tracy asked. "Wouldn't it be safer?"

"Probably," Shane answered for him. "And if this was a union shoot, we'd have to. We can get away with a lot more on an indie production. Sy knows that, and he likes to cut corners whenever he can. It keeps the costs down."

"I heard we're not going to come in under budget anyway," Gus said, looking over his shoulder.

"Sy will hit the roof if that's true. He was just complaining to me that some of the dailies had to be reshot. The lighting was off."

"He'll be murder to deal with," Crystal said acidly. "Even more unpleasant than usual. The head office will come down hard on him, and he'll take it out on us. If there was any way he could cut our already paltry salaries down to minimum-wage, he would. This is the chance you take when you work for a sleazy operation like Fearless Productions. I should have known better." She glanced at Tracy. "You're not writing all this down, are you, hon? Because everything we're saying here is off the record." She glanced around the table. "We should have spelled that out earlier, you know?"

Gus flushed. "I never even thought of that. Tracy, honey, forget what I just said. Especially the part about using extras instead of pros for the stunts. You could cost me my job." He gave a nervous laugh and wiped his palms on his already grungy jeans.

"Then you'd be back to washing cars for a living," Crystal said nastily.

"I wasn't washing cars!" Gus said in an aggrieved tone. "I managed a whole fleet of vehicles for a movie company! Why do you always put the worst possible spin on everything? Didn't your mother teach you that if you can't say something nice about someone, don't say anything at all?"

"It's part of my charm," Crystal said, looking bored. "You should know that by now, Gus."

"Uh, Tracy, you're really not going to spill the beans on us, are you?" Gus seemed to pale under his sunburn.

"Of course not. I'm not writing anything down, see?" Tracy smiled and held up her hands. "I'm not trying to spill any secrets, honest. I'm just doing a video diary for extra credit in my English class."

"She's perfectly harmless," Heidi piped up. "Why don't you give the kid a break?"

"Let's hope those shots never get any further than your scrapbook, sweetie," Crystal said. "I've gotta tell you, you've managed to make a few enemies here, you know. No one wants to be photographed sleeping on the job."

"Sleeping on the job?" Tracy wrinkled her brow, puzzled.

Gus laughed. "Yeah, I saw you take some shots of Sandy snoozing under the tree the other day on the back lot. He thought he'd catch a few winks, but you jolted him awake."

"Gosh, I didn't mean to do anything wrong," Tracy said, her voice quavering. "It was just a really cute shot of Sandy lying in the grass with his cowboy hat over his face. I was going to make copies for everyone when the shoot is over. I thought you'd all like to have a souvenir of your time at Fairmont."

"A souvenir is one thing, sweetie," Crystal said tightly. "A tabloid spread is another. You'd be surprised what some people would do for money." She shot Gus a death glare as he stuffed himself with barbecue, oblivious to her withering look. "They'd sell their own mother for a buck, that's what they'd do." She glanced around the table, looking disappointed when no one stepped in to agree with her.

Lu Anne joined us then, and the conversation shifted to safer topics. I saw Crystal give Tracy a sharp look a few times, as if she wondered what was really behind this video diary project. She didn't really think Tracy had connections with one of the tabloids, did she? I remembered Shane's warning about *StarGazer*. Maybe he was right to be paranoid. Maybe the tabloid was planning some sort of hatchet job on him, a story full of lies and half-truths. As Lu Anne said once, "Just because you're paranoid doesn't mean they're not out to get you."

Chapter Nine

⭐

"HERE IT IS! WE'RE IN LUCK!" I GRABBED THE LAST COPY OF *StarGazer* from the magazine rack in the convenience store on Main Street. It was late afternoon, and since production had wrapped early, I had invited Tracy back to my house for a major heart-to-heart. She still hadn't found her digital camera, and I wanted to tell her all about the scene in Shane's trailer.

And she didn't know anything about the phone call from Marc in New Orleans! How could I have forgotten that? I felt a little pang, remembering how close we had been in New Orleans last summer, and how time and distance had separated us.

"I have to make a quick stop," I'd said, pushing her into the

7-Eleven. "I'll get us some sodas." I was really stopping because I just had to see that tabloid article Shane told me about. How bad could it be? I wondered. I remembered Crystal Hall saying, "Any publicity is good publicity." Could that really be true? Shane had seemed pretty upset about the feature on him, and I wondered what they had come up with. What was he afraid of? He had a reputation in Hollywood for being as squeaky clean as Clay Aiken. Or had someone blown his cover?

"Are you sure this is the right paper?" Tracy asked, as we headed out of the store into the waning sunlight. "It says, 'Space Aliens Land in Georgia,' " she said with a giggle. "And look at this one. 'Sexy Supermodel Is Actually 103 Years Old.' "

"This is the right paper," I said firmly. "Look, there's Shane's picture in a little circle on the bottom of the cover." It was next to a photo of a chihuahua who spoke seven languages.

"Are you sure this is Shane?" Tracy squinted at the grainy black-and-white photograph. "It could be any tall, good-looking dude in a cowboy hat." SHANE'S NIGHT ON THE TOWN! the headline screamed. I could hardly wait to read the whole story.

"It might not even be him," Tracy said twenty minutes later. We were sitting in my back garden, flipping though the *StarGazer*, looking for any other mention of Shane. The article portrayed Shane Rockett as a major sleaze, a love 'em and leave 'em type who frequented Hollywood parties with a girl on each arm. All the shots seemed a little out of focus, and I wondered if Tracy could be right. Maybe it wasn't Shane after all. The Q and A section was mostly a warmed-over version of other interviews, the same questions about how Shane got into show business, what he eats for break-fast, and if he answers his own fan mail. I was beginning to wonder if the reporter had actually interviewed Shane or just done a "cut-and-paste" job, putting together lots of old clippings.

"You know, if half of these things were true, I would never want to see Shane again," I told Tracy. I had already confided to Tracy about the brief kiss in the trailer, leaving out the fact that I had nearly fainted from excitement. "It makes him sound like all he does is hang around Sunset Strip every night, looking for the wildest party he can find. Here he is standing outside The Snake Pit, with some bimbo attached to him like Velcro."

Tracy frowned. "The Snake Pit?" She grabbed the paper for a closer look. "Jessie, I think I read they closed The Snake Pit. It's very possible none of this is really true. Maybe it's all a setup. And I'm not even sure the guy in the picture is re-ally Shane." She paused. "If you have any doubts, why don't you just ask him?"

Trust Tracy to be direct. Maybe I didn't want to ask him

because I didn't want to let on that it mattered to me? Plus how would I explain that I had bought one of those "trashy tabloids"? Shane would think of it as the ultimate betrayal, wouldn't he?

I managed a weak laugh. "Tracy, Shane is not only a babe, he's a major movie star. Why do you think he'd tell me the truth? And why is it any of my business? After all, I'm just a bit player on a movie he happens to be working on. That's the way he would look at it."

"Don't underestimate yourself," Tracy said. "If Shane really cares about you, he'd want to set the record straight. In fact, he'd insist on it. Trust me."

I thought about the passionate, feathery kisses in the trailer. Shane had said he wanted to get to know me, that he was going to tell me all his secrets. "I wonder if it's all a joke?" I said to Tracy. She didn't answer right away, and she was staring behind me, as if she had seen a ghost. She opened and closed her mouth like a landed goldfish. "Tracy, what's wrong?" I said, alarmed. "I asked you if you thought this was all a joke."

"This isn't a joke," I heard my mother say laughingly. "Jessie, turn around. There's a big surprise waiting for you."

"A surprise? What kind of a—" I never got to finish the sentence, because there, standing behind Mom, tall, dark and babelicious, was the biggest surprise of my life.

Marc LaPierre.

"Marc!" I scrambled to my feet and we ran down the flagstone path to greet each other. I found myself wrapped in Marc's embrace, holding on for dear life as he laughed and swung me around like I was a rag doll.

"What are you doing here?" I gasped when he finally put me down. He looked terrific, in tan chinos and a white Abercrombie shirt that emphasized his strong shoulders and broad chest. He had a healthy Louisiana tan and his dark eyes sparkled with excitement. His hair was a little longer, cut in a kind of shaggy Brad Pitt style that made him look even hotter than I remembered. Plus he had this sexy New Orleans accent. Who can resist a guy who calls you *cher*?

"What am I doing here? What kind of greeting is that?" he teased me. "I flew standby just to see you! I was crammed into a middle seat in coach between two enormous women with shopping bags. And one of them ate an entire pepperoni pizza right in front of me. She had brought it on board with her. I guess she knew all they were going to serve were cocktail peanuts and Goldfish crackers."

"I didn't mean it that way," I said, flushing. "I'm just surprised, that's all. I thought you were going to use your mom's frequent-flyer miles to get up here. I figured it would take weeks to arrange it."

"There were so many blackout dates, it was impossible to get a round-trip ticket," he said, sinking into an Adirondack chair. "A standby spot opened up, and I grabbed it.

I can only stay overnight, though. I have to leave tomorrow afternoon after lunch. I've got a seat on a flight out of Bedford at five-thirty. Your mom has been nice enough to offer me a lift to the airport."

"Well, a quick trip is better than nothing," Tracy piped up. Tracy had met Marc last summer in New Orleans and had always liked him.

"Hey, Tracy," he said, suddenly noticing her. "Good to see you."

"You, too." She grinned back at him.

"Did Jessie tell you I was coming up here for a visit?"

Tracy looked him straight in the eye. "I'm not gonna lie to you, Marc." She paused dramatically. "That's all she's been talking about!"

"I'm glad to hear it," he said, shooting me a look that made my heart skip a beat.

"I've got iced tea and brownies," Mom said, holding a tray. Marc immediately jumped up to help her. "Why, thank you, Marc." She looked happy to see him. "Your mother raised you to be a perfect gentleman." She started passing out raspberry iced tea and little napkins, while Marc followed with the brownies. "How is she doing, by the way?"

"Very well," Marc said, sitting down again. "She sends her best. Things at The Black Swan have been very busy. We've added a Sunday evening chocolate buffet and it really keeps things hopping. People come in for dessert and coffee around eight or eight-thirty and we serve it under the umbrella tables. It's very popular and the food critic for the *Times* even did a feature on it."

"A chocolate buffet," Mom exclaimed. "What a great idea. I remember what a beautiful setting you have, all those lovely willows in the back."

"SO YOU'RE TAKING MARC TO THE SET WITH YOU TOMORROW?" my mother asked. "I know he's dying to see it."

"I think so," I said hesitantly. "Marc, I'm not sure what the rules are about bringing visitors to the set. I know I can't just show up with you without permission, and I'm not really sure how to handle it. I'll have to ask Lu Anne first, don't you think?" I asked Tracy. "Or should I go directly to Sy?" The thought of approaching Sy Templeton filled me with a sick feeling in the pit of my stomach. I could just picture him peering at me in that owlish fashion, over his horn-rimmed glasses, all ready to bark "No!" at me. If only Marc had given me some notice, I could have figured all this out. I was happy to see Marc, but it was hard not to feel annoyed at his impulsiveness.

Tracy raised her eyebrows, considering. "I'd ask Lu Anne before I'd ask Sy. If you catch Sy in a bad mood, he's murder. Lu Anne's bad enough," she said fervently.

Marc shot me a blank look, and I giggled. "Oh, sorry.

I forgot you don't know any of these people. Sy is the director of the film, and Lu Anne is the Continuity girl, but she
seems to run everything. They've worked together for a long
time, and she practically reads Sy's mind. Lu Anne's okay,
but I don't have a great relationship with Sy." I thought of
telling Marc how I flubbed my lines the very first day, and
decided not to. Better let him keep a few illusions about me!

"I hope it won't be a problem getting me past the front
gate," Marc said, looking crestfallen. "I've never been on a
movie set before." He looked so downcast, I was beginning
to wonder if Marc had really come to see me, or to fulfill a
lifetime dream of mixing with movie stars!

"I'm sure we can work it out," Tracy said, ever the opti-
mist. "In fact, you know what you could do, Jessie? You
could ask Heidi Hopkins if you can bring Marc with you.
That would be even better than asking Lu Anne. One word
from Heidi Hopkins and Sy jumps through hoops. She's a
major star and she's got a lot of power. When she's happy,
he's happy."

"That's a wonderful idea, Tracy." Mom passed around the
brownie tray, urging everyone to have more. "Heidi is such a
lovely girl, I'm sure she wouldn't mind putting in a good
word for Marc."

"Do you know Heidi Hopkins? I mean, personally?"
Marc was leaning forward eagerly, and my worst suspicions
were confirmed. The guy was acting like a male groupie!

"We had her over for dinner," Mom confided. "And you know something, Marc? She's just as down to earth as she can be. She told us all about her movie career, and how she started out in the road company of *Annie*. She hasn't had an easy life, and I'm glad to see that the poor girl has finally made it to the top." Mom laughed. "You wouldn't believe some of the Hollywood stories she told us. Once she accidentally set her hair on fire during a dinner party scene in a big movie. She bent over the centerpiece and forgot someone had lit the candles in the arrangement." She turned to me. "Heidi has a real knack for telling stories, doesn't she? She said Shane Rockett came to her rescue. He put out the fire with his bare hands, and only the ends of her hair were singed. It was hilarious the way she described it, wasn't it, Jessie?"

"Hilarious," I said tightly, wishing I could nudge the conversation on to other topics. Anything but Heidi Hopkins. Marc was sitting on the edge of his seat and from the light in his eyes, I could see a Major Crush forming. Even sight unseen, Heidi Hopkins seemed to exert a magic power over him. What would happen when he met her in person?

"She set her hair on fire during a movie shoot? Wow, I would have given anything to have heard that story." Marc sounded so excited, you'd think he'd missed a front-row seat at a Britney Spears concert. "Maybe I'll be able to sit down with her tomorrow for a few minutes. Do you think she'd agree to see me? Or maybe have her picture taken with me?"

"Don't get carried away," I said wryly. "We have a really busy shooting schedule. There's not much downtime on a movie set. You'll see that for yourself." *If I can manage to sneak him past Sy and his watchdog, Lu Anne*, I thought.

Marc offered to take us all out to dinner later that evening, but Mom said the garden was so pretty, we should just order pizza and eat on the patio. The evening really brought back old times. Marc was just as funny and charming as I remembered, telling stories about New Orleans and the guests at The Black Swan.

Much later, Marc and I were finally alone. Tracy had gone home, and Mom had discreetly vanished inside, saying she had some paperwork to do in her office. She smiled at us, and I could read her thoughts. She figured I wanted some time alone with Marc.

The air was soft and humid, the garden shrouded in shadows. Cicadas chattered in the trees, the velvety black sky was sprinkled with stars, and an owl hooted somewhere in the distance. If we were shooting a movie, this would be the perfect romantic setting, I decided. Except my thoughts kept drifting back to Shane, no matter how hard I tried to focus on Marc.

"So here we are," Marc said. He reached over and took my hand, his dark eyes flashing. His grip was strong and warm, as his fingers curled around mine. "Have you missed me, *cher*?

Because I've missed you every single day." *Cher* is short for *cherie*, a French word for "darling."

For just a moment, I flashed on Shane calling me "dar-lin'" earlier that day. Was it just a coincidence? Shane Rock-ett and Marc LaPierre, two dynamite guys, both drop-dead gorgeous, both using the same term of endearment. I smiled, thinking of Tracy, who didn't believe in coincidences. She would say it was fate, that my moon must be in retrograde or Aquarius was on the cusp, and that's why the cosmos was throwing these delicious goodies my way. I didn't really care about the explanation. Fate or coincidence, I was experienc-ing very good karma!

"I've missed you *more*. I've missed you night and day," I said teasingly, letting Marc pull me close to him on the glider. I tucked my legs under me and nestled against his strong shoulder. He leaned close to nuzzle my neck and I inhaled the clean, spicy scent of his aftershave.

"Except when you're signing autographs, of course. And when you're practicing your Academy Awards speech. Gee, wonder if you'll get a star on the Hollywood Walk of Fame?" he kidded me. "After all, you're a big movie star now. The next thing I know, you'll be on the cover of *Teen People*."

"Stop that," I said. I tossed a pillow at him, but he laughed and ducked just in time. "You know that's not true. I've got a teeny-tiny part in the movie. You'll see for yourself tomorrow when we visit the set." I didn't tell him my part was much bigger than it was in the original version, or that all my new scenes were with Shane. And I wasn't thrilled at the idea of Shane meeting Marc. For some reason, I wanted to keep Shane and Marc in two separate compartments. Was it because I was attracted to both of them?

I was relieved when Mom called me inside for a phone call a few minutes later. It was Heidi, asking if she had left her sunglasses at our house that night at dinner. When I explained that Marc wanted to visit the set in the morning, she promised to take care of it. I found her sunglasses on the hall table, and before we hung up, she even offered to pose for a picture with Marc. She seemed pleased at Marc's arrival, and I wondered if she had thought I was competing with her for Shane. But then I decided that was nuts. Anyone who looked like Heidi Hopkins couldn't possibly think of me as competition, could she?

"It's all set. You'll get a guest pass, no problem-o." I rejoined Marc on the glider and told him about the conversation with Heidi. I deliberately left out her offer to pose for a picture with him. He was already salivating just at the thought of meeting her—why should I send his testosterone soaring into overdrive by telling him he could have his picture taken with her?

And then he was off and running. What was Heidi really like? Was she dating anyone? Was it true that she carried her pet chihuahua everywhere with her in a two-thousand-dollar dog carrier? I felt a little hurt, wondering how to deflect this Heidi marathon, when he suddenly pulled me into his arms and kissed me. "I've been wanting to do that ever since I got here," he said softly.

The skin tingled on the back of my neck. Shane had said the exact same words in his trailer, earlier that day! I stiffened, and Marc turned his sexy dark eyes on me, questioningly. "What's wrong, Jess?" His voice was low and husky, full of longing.

"Nothing," I said, trying to shrug off the memory of Shane. "I'm just tired, it's been a long day."

He rubbed the back of my neck and I thought of all the good times we had spent together last summer. "You seem different, Jessie," he said, his dark eyes troubled. "Is it just because we haven't seen each other in a while, or is it something else?"

I faked a yawn and shook my head. "No, it's nothing. I told you, I'm just wiped out. We've only been shooting for a few days, and I'm already caught up in a mystery. I'm beginning to feel like Sherlock Holmes."

"What kind of mystery?"

"A robbery, but there's more to it than that. Tracy's camera is missing, and she thinks somebody might have swiped it. It turns out that not everyone on the set is thrilled having a roving reporter taking pictures. I've heard a few people say that Tracy is Bedford's version of the paparazzi."

"They really said that about her? You'd think movie stars would be used to being photographed all the time. And it seems like a stretch to think that someone would actually steal her camera. What do you think's going on?" He slid his hand down my arm, pulling me close again.

"I don't know what to think," I said hesitantly. "I'm getting some bad vibes from the crew members, and things are a little tense on the set. But would someone go so far as to steal the camera?" I shook my head. "I just don't know. It's a mystery."

"Well, Jessie, if anyone can figure out what's going on, you can." He buried his face in my hair. "Maybe I can help you figure it out. We made a good team last summer, didn't we?" Marc seemed to be deliberately talking about the past as a way of reconnecting with me now.

I didn't have to come up with an answer, because Mom stepped out of the darkness just then, startling us both. "Shall I light the citronella candles? The mosquitos will eat you alive out here."

I jumped up, eager to have an excuse to flee the garden. I wasn't in the mood for an intimate tête-à-tête with Marc. My thoughts were confused, and my heart was torn in two directions. I'm a Pisces, and it's not surprising that my sign is two fishes swimming in opposite directions. That's exactly the way I felt. Torn and conflicted, at a loss what to do next. Marc and Shane, two great guys, one real and one a Hollywood fantasy. Marc was available, here and now, and he'd flown a thousand miles to see me. That should be the deciding factor, shouldn't it? Wrong. My traitorous heart knew what it wanted . . . it wanted the fantasy.

It wanted Shane Rockett.

"Don't bother with the candles, Mom. We're just going inside now anyway." I faked another yawn. At the rate I was going, Marc would think I had narcolepsy. He looked a little disappointed but stood up, ready to follow me.

"Are you sure?" Mom sounded apologetic, as she gathered up the coffee cups. She probably thought she had interrupted the beginnings of a major make-out session.

"I'm positive," I said, too heartily. "We're going to have some more of those dynamite brownies and then I think I'll have to say good night. I've got an early call tomorrow." I turned to Marc. "Don't forget, we both have to leave the house no later than six."

"Oh. Well, okay then," she said uncertainly. She knew I was a night owl and raised her eyebrows, sending me one of her what-is-going-on looks. I knew she was baffled that I didn't want to spend more private time with Marc. "I already have your bed turned down, Marc, and you have clean towels on the dresser. If you need anything else, just tell me."

"Thanks, Mrs. P. I think I'll join Jessie for a quick snack and then hit the sack myself. It's been a long day."

Chapter Ten

⭐

"IS THERE TROUBLE ON THE SET?" MOM ASKED HALF AN HOUR later. Marc had already turned in, and we were closing up the house for the night.

"Something's going on, but I'm not sure exactly what," I confessed. Mom had overheard the crack about Tracy being as annoying as the "paparazzi" and wanted to hear more. "It's true that Tracy's made a few enemies by taking some candid shots, but she doesn't seem to realize it."

"What's wrong with her taking some candid shots? I thought she had permission."

"Technically, she does, but let's face it. Movie stars don't like being caught off guard. They tend to be control freaks, and they like to control any publicity that goes out, especially pictures of themselves. The last thing they'd want is a really lousy, unflattering shot ending up on the cover of *StarGazer*."

Mom poured herself a cup of chamomile tea and stared at me in surprise. "Well, no one would do that, would they?"

I shook my head. "No, you're right, it's crazy. I'm sure they're worrying for nothing. Actors tend to be paranoid, and I'm getting just as bad, hanging around with them."

"WHOEVER DID THIS IS HISTORY! SY WILL HAVE HIS HEAD ON A platter! He'll never work in movies again, Sy will see to that," Lu Anne muttered the next morning. Marc and I had just arrived on the set, and were heading for the breakfast table. The sun was rising in a robin's-egg sky and I could tell it was going to be another perfect day. Everyone looked happy and relaxed, except for Lu Anne, who was stomping around in her Doc Martens, grimly waving a tabloid. "I'm telling you"—she said to no one in particular—"someone's gonna pay for this! You got that? Big-time!"

"What in the world—" Heidi began.

"Here, sweetie, read it for yourself." Lu Anne shoved the paper at Heidi and eyeballed the cluster of actors and crew drinking coffee. "Looks like we have a spy in our midst, folks. Or should I say, a rat! And I'm gonna flush this rat right down the drain—you can bet on it!"

"Lu Anne, take it easy, girl," Gus said, lumbering over.

"You sound meaner than a rattlesnake, and I haven't even had my caffeine fix yet. So tell me, sweetheart, what's got you in a dander?" Gus was balancing two jelly donuts on top of a paper cup of coffee, looking for a place to sit down.

"You think I sound mean?" Lu Anne said, challenging. "You don't know mean until you see what Sy does when he reads this. Come to think of it, he won't be mean, he'll go ballistic!"

"Wow, you better take a look at this, Gus. Lu Anne's right. It's pretty bad." Heidi said. "The headline says: 'Asleep at the Switch.' It's written by someone named Rick Morgan. Check out the picture. There's Sandy snoozing under a tree, but the article says he's passed out dead drunk. And uh-oh, here's something about you, Gus."

"Yeah? I've got my name in print?" Gus put down the coffee and donuts to tuck his faded flannel shirt into his jeans. "You know what they say, Joe," he said, nudging a bored-looking cameraman, "any publicity is good publicity."

"Um, not this time, Gus." Heidi frowned. "It says you're using untrained people to do stunts, because you're too cheap to pay for professionals. And oh, no . . . listen to this. It says you're in big trouble with the law, and the attorney general's office is going to start an investigation. Apparently it's a criminal offense to put amateurs in dangerous situations on the job."

"Dangerous situations? What are they talking about? That's

crazy! Where do they get this stuff from?" Gus suddenly snapped to attention, abandoning his kindly Grizzly Adams act. "Gimme that paper!" he thundered. I hurried over and peered over Heidi's shoulder as he grabbed the paper out of her hands. I only managed to read a few lines, but Heidi was right. It looked like *StarGazer* had really nailed Fearless Productions.

Gus was so upset, his hands were trembling. "I can't read this without my glasses," he said, handing it to me. I quickly scanned the rest of the article. It was very bad. There was Tracy's picture of Sandy, sleeping in the grass with a cowboy hat shading his face. He was wearing a Fearless T-shirt, and you could see the extras milling around in the background, waiting for the next shot.

"It looks like an empty bottle of whiskey in the picture," I pointed out. "Right next to Sandy's hand."

"Oh no," Heidi said. "Look, Gus, she's right." She stuck the paper under his nose. "They want people to think he passed out, dead drunk."

"They sure do, the scumbags! You've got sharp eyes, girl," Gus told me. "I don't know how they got that bottle there. Maybe one of the guys put it there as a joke—"

"Or it was computer-generated," Marc spoke up. Everyone turned to look at him. "It's easy to add something that wasn't in the original picture. Sometimes you can tell if you look carefully at the edges of the object. The edges are a dead giveaway. They never look quite right, if you insert something into the picture." He paused, looking a little embarrassed at the sudden silence. "You can tell I spend a lot of time fooling around with computers." He laughed, breaking the tension.

Heidi looked him over from head to toe. Never missing an opportunity to impress a cute guy, she stuck out her hand. "Hi, there. I'm Heidi Hopkins. And you don't look like a computer geek to me."

"Marc LaPierre," he said, stepping forward with a killer smile. "I'm here with Jessie." I felt a glow of pride as several extras turned to stare at me. Marc had created a little buzz when we arrived together earlier that morning. A few of the extras had thought he was some hot new actor from Holly-wood and tried to strike up a conversation with him. He had just grinned and shown them his guest pass. I had kid-ded him that maybe he was the next Josh Hartnett.

"You're the New Orleans guy!" Heidi said with sudden recognition.

"I've never thought of myself that way," Marc said with a grin, "but yes, I suppose I am." He looked pleased at her at-tention, and a little flame of jealousy flickered inside me. If I wasn't careful, I'd make some nasty comment that I would regret later.

"Well, I'm sorry you're seeing us in the middle of a big crisis," she said, flashing him a Hollywood smile. "We're usually a pretty laid-back group. Except for Miss Drama Queen over there." She lowered her voice and nodded toward Lu Anne, who was screaming at someone on her cell phone.

Lu Anne was still on the rampage. "I'm telling you I don't know how that picture got in there. And I can't find Tracy, so I can't ask her. Don't you think I would, if I could?" Her voice spiraled skyward, in a supersonic shriek, and Marc flinched.

"*Cher*, what's going on?" he murmured. "Has Tracy done something?"

"It's okay," I assured him. "Lu Anne is like Vesuvius. She erupts every hour on the hour." I managed a light laugh. "It's nothing, believe me. We've all learned to ignore it. She'll simmer down in a few minutes."

"Not this time," Heidi said darkly. "This is big time. Sy's been in trouble with the Labor Department before, and the last thing he needs is the film commission getting wind of this. They could force him to close down production, right in the middle of the movie. Where is Tracy, anyway?" she said, looking around. "I haven't seen her all morning. Is she lying low someplace?"

"Of course not," I said firmly. "Tracy had nothing to do with this photograph, so she has nothing to be embarrassed about." Privately, I wondered what was keeping Tracy. We had come to the set separately that morning, but had agreed to meet at noon for lunch. My mom was picking Marc up later to drive him to the airport, so this would be the last chance we had to see him before he headed back to New Orleans.

"And I'm sure Tracy'll be glad to explain it all when she gets here," Gus said darkly. He was pacing nervously, his hands thrust in his jeans pockets, his coffee and donuts forgotten. "How did that picture get in *StarGazer?* That's what I'd like to know. Someone must have sent it to them. And money must have changed hands. Not just a few bucks, I'm talking big money."

"Oh, money always changes hands, doesn't it, Gus? That's what makes the world go round." I turned to see Crystal Hall weaving her way to the breakfast buffet. She stopped to glance at the paper I was still holding. "So, it's true? Sandy was passed out drunk and somebody took his picture? What a hoot!"

"No, it's not true," Gus said sharply. "Only someone with an evil mind would think so. Someone like you, Crystal."

"What did you say?" Crystal turned suddenly, nearly knocking over the coffeepot. "An evil mind?" When Gus didn't answer, she cackled. "It looks like you've finally gotten yourself some publicity, Gus. Not quite what you expected, though, was it?"

I frowned, wondering about their relationship. Every time I saw Gus and Crystal together, they seemed to be arguing. Did they just happen to rub each other the wrong way, or was there some history there that I didn't know about?

"None of it's true," Gus muttered unhappily. "Not a word of it."

"Oh, but it doesn't matter if something's true or not," Crystal said, shooting him a sharp look. "All that really matters is what Sy will think about it. That's what show business is all about. Right, sweetie?" She leaned close to him, smiling. "I think I'll go talk to Lu Anne and find out what the latest is. Don't go anywhere, darlings. I'll be right back with all the gossip."

"That woman!" Gus exploded. "It's time for her to retire. She poisons every set she's on. Why doesn't Sy see through her?"

"Oh, I'm sure he does," Heidi said. "But she's getting so old, she'll grab any job, and Sy probably pays her the minimum. As far as retiring, I bet she'd pay him for the chance to keep on working. She told me once she wants to work forever. She doesn't want to end up in that retirement home they have for old actors in Hollywood."

"We all have to stop working, sometime," Gus said. "I won't be able to work much longer if my back gives out. The doc tells me it could happen any day now." He looked around to see if anyone wanted to hear more about his ailing back, and his jowly face sagged in disappointment when he was met with dead silence.

"I'm afraid you picked the wrong day to visit the set," Heidi said, eyeing Marc. She couldn't seem to take her eyes off him, and she leaned forward, giving him a great view of her cleavage in her pink camisole top. "Maybe you can come back when all this has settled down, and everyone's in a better mood." She tossed her blond hair over her shoulder and posed with one long, tanned leg in front of the other, model-style.

Marc smiled and took my hand, locking my fingers in his. "I'm afraid that's impossible. I'm flying back to New Orleans today. This was just a surprise visit, wasn't it, Jessie?" I nodded, feeling a little glow of pleasure. "Next time, it will be Jessie's turn to come to New Orleans."

The morning passed quickly, and Marc chuckled, watching Lu Anne moving the extras back and forth in position for the shots. "She's just like a Border collie, herding them like sheep," he whispered to me. He looked very handsome, his black hair gleaming in the sunlight. I was torn. He was going back to New Orleans in just a few hours, and I still hadn't told him about Shane. Nothing was settled between us, and I wondered if I was making the biggest mistake of my life.

"Believe me, if she could nip at their heels, she would," I whispered back. We laughed together, and suddenly the awkwardness faded, and for a moment it was like old times again.

We didn't catch up with Tracy until lunchtime, and she surprised me by waving her camera triumphantly in the air.

"I got it back! You're not gonna believe where it was!" I quickly pushed her ahead of me in line before anyone could object. "Maisie spotted it in the lost and found. She pulled it out and gave it to me."

"Forget about the camera! Don't you know everyone's been looking for you?" I pulled her close, and said in a low voice, "They're wondering if you know how that picture of Sandy got in *StarGazer*. That's all anyone's been talking about. And the fact that someone spilled the beans about using untrained people to do stunt work."

"Oh that," Tracy said, shrugging. "Sy and I had a talk about that. It's okay, he knows I didn't have anything to do with it. He was really cool about it."

"He was?" I wasn't prepared to see Mad Dog Sy as a friendly, sympathetic creature. I couldn't have been more surprised if Tracy had said Sy had morphed into the Easter Bunny.

"He doesn't hold me the tiniest bit responsible," Tracy said earnestly. "He knows it wasn't my fault. It's just one of those things that happened, and he said not to worry about it. He'll get to the bottom of it, believe me. He's going to track down the reporter, Rick Morgan, and confront him."

"But what really happened? How did the photo get to the tabloids? Somebody must have sold it. And who leaked the information that extras were going to be doing stunts in the chase scene? Who would know all that?"

"Sy said he has his suspicions. But you know something?" Tracy gave an impish grin, her eyes sparkling. "I think he likes me. He told me he knows I would never do anything to hurt the production. And Lu Anne hinted that she knows who did it. She said that some people will do anything for money."

"Wow, is that a hundred-and-eighty-degree turn, or what!" I looked over the lunch selections and piled a Caesar salad on my plate. "I was sure they were gong to blame you. Here I've been worrying about you all morning for nothing."

"So have I," Marc piped up. "We thought you were really in for it. Lu Anne was promising to decapitate someone over that article."

"Nope, everything's cool." She glanced at Lu Anne rushing by with her clipboard, barking into her cell phone as usual. "But when the truth comes out, I bet somebody's going to be in big trouble with Sy and Lu Anne. I'm just glad it's not me."

Lunch was quiet and uneventful. Tracy started to edge away with her tray, as if she planned on leaving me alone with Marc, but I insisted she join us at a tiny table under the elm trees, away from the set.

The truth is, I didn't want to eat lunch with Marc by myself. I was glad to see him, but things had been a little tense last night, and there was still a cloud of uncertainty hanging between us. I know I had hurt Marc by acting lukewarm about his visit, but I couldn't focus when Shane kept drifting into my mind. Sexy, charismatic Shane with his bedroom eyes and killer smile. One look from him and I was hooked.

We hung around chatting with the stunt crew after lunch. They were planning the big chase scene at the diner later that day, and Marc hung on their every word, enjoying the demonstration. Gus showed him a series of diagrams, explaining that he always carried a stopwatch, and everything was choreographed to the second. It would look like complete chaos, cars zooming everywhere at high speeds with plenty of near crashes, but actually everything would be carefully blocked and rehearsed. According to Gus, it was safer than driving on the interstate.

At one point, Shane came over and introduced himself. Marc nodded coolly, seemingly unimpressed. Did he sense something was going on between us? Shane must have sensed a chill in the air, because he sidled away, tipping his hat, with a brief, "Later, Jess." At least he didn't call me "darlin'," which I knew would have put Marc, already suspicious, on red alert.

"Later? What was that all about?" A flicker of annoyance crossed Marc's handsome features and he gave Shane a hard stare as he ambled back to the set.

"It's nothing, we're in the chase scene together later today," I said too quickly. I smiled as if to convince Marc that being in a movie scene with the hottest male star in the country meant nothing to me. "I wasn't even supposed to be in the scene, but they suddenly decided it made more sense in terms of the plot." I was suddenly relieved that Marc would be gone by the time we started filming the scene. I would have felt awkward having him watch me acting with Shane, even though it was strictly an action scene, and not the least bit romantic.

"I don't like the idea," Marc said slowly. "Jessie, be careful. These guys are professionals, they're trained to do high-speed chases. They think nothing of turning over cars or jumping over barricades. But it's no place for you. There's always the possibility of being hurt, no matter how many precautions they take."

"Don't worry, I'm not going to be the one driving," I told him. I was touched that he was worried about me. If only I hadn't met Shane, everything would have been different between us. "All I have to do is sit in the passenger seat. And you saw for yourself, the cars are well padded inside."

This wasn't just brave talk—I really wasn't worried. Gus had shown us one of the stunt cars, and the whole dashboard was covered with thick foam with heavy quilted pads underneath. "We'll strap you in as tight as we can with the lap belts. You'll be as safe as can be, I'll make sure of it."

Mom pulled up then, at the circle in front of the main building. She kept the car idling, while Marc and I walked across the lawn to her. He grabbed my hand, locking his fingers through mine and my mind swirled with a million things I wanted to say to him.

"I can't believe it's time for you to go," I said, surprising myself by feeling a little weepy. I pressed my lips together to fight the wave of emotion I felt. Marc was still the same terrific person he had always been. It wasn't his fault that Shane had swept into my life like a tornado, taking over my heart in one fell swoop.

"This is good-bye for a while," he said sadly. "I'm going to miss you, *cher*."

"Me, too," I told him. My heart melted a little when he ducked his head to give me a quick kiss. Just for a moment, my heart thudded, remembering everything we had meant to each other. But that was last summer and Shane was in my life now. I hugged him tightly, aware of the extras staring with open curiosity. "Call me tonight to let me know you got home safely."

"I'll call you to make sure you survived the chase scene," he said with a wan smile. "I just hope this isn't going to be the start of a new career for you. I can see it now. Jessie Phillips, stuntwoman to the stars."

"Don't worry, that's not going to happen. I don't feel like being bruised from head to toe. Say hi to your parents for me," I told him, as he climbed in the front seat next to Mom.

Tracy and I stood there waving until the car disappeared

down the long winding driveway to Main Street. I felt a little lump rising in my throat, and willed it to disappear.
Time to move on, I told myself, but for some reason, I was
rooted to the spot.

Jessie, get a hold of yourself, I said. This was no time for
soppy emotion. I had a busy afternoon ahead of me. I still
had to rehearse my line for the chase scene, talk to Gus
about the blocking, and get together with Maisie about my
costume. I was wearing a flirty little sundress with strappy
sandals, and I needed to have a quick fitting. And I needed
a special appointment with Hair because they decided I
should wear my hair in a French braid so it wouldn't blow
around in the open car. Plus a trip to Arnie in Makeup. But
suddenly none of that mattered. I felt rooted to the spot,
staring down the empty driveway, feeling utterly alone,
overwhelmed by sadness.

It suddenly felt so final. Marc was gone.

"I think he knows," Tracy said quietly.

"Knows what?" I was still staring after the car, thinking
about all the hopes and dreams I had once had about Marc.
I blinked fast, feeling hot tears behind my eyes.

"That you're crazy in love with Shane."

*Leave it to your best friend to tell you what you don't want
to hear.* "Tracy, I'm not even sure what I think at the moment—" I began, but she cut me off.

"Don't even start with me, Jessie," she said, waving her

hand dismissively "I can read your mind, remember? And I know a major crush when I see one. Shane's the only guy in the world for you, I can tell."

"Do you really think so?"

"I know you think so." The afternoon sun was beating down as we started to walk back over the carefully manicured lawn to the set. "I just hope you've made the right choice."

Chapter Eleven

★

"WE'RE GOING TO DO A RUN-THROUGH FIRST," SANDY SHOUTED through the megaphone. "Everybody remember to hit their marks at the right time, that's all you have to do. We're not even going to use the cameras, I just want to get a rough idea of the timing."

"And we want to make sure everyone ends up at the right place at the right time. Move in as tight as you can, but no crashes and no fender benders!" Gus shouted. Gus was dressed in full motorcycle regalia, complete with a headband that made him look like Andre Agassi.

According to the script, Gus and his motorcycle gang were terrorizing a small Southern town and Shane, a bounty hunter, had tracked them to the local diner. When the bikers were confronted by Shane, they turned tail and sped down the highway. Natalie, my character, was riding along with Shane because her sister was missing, and she thought the gang might have kidnapped her.

"Is everyone clear on their cues?" Gus shouted. "Ned and Russell," he pointed to two overweight stuntmen on hogs, "you're going to pull in from the south side of the road, just as the tour bus is leaving. I want you to almost sideswipe them on the left side, you got that? I want it close enough it looks realistic, but no scrapes. Don't take any chances."

Both men, dressed from head to toe in black leather, gave Gus a thumbs-up. "Roger," the taller of the pair said. "We'll come as close as we can."

"And no showin' off," Gus reminded them. "No wheelies, just get to the right place at the right time, that's all I ask. Now, Shane, are you straight on what you're doing?"

"I pull up fast in front of the diner, throw up a little gravel, then do a one-eighty and head down the highway once the guys come busting out of the front door."

"That's right." Gus saw me standing next to Shane. "Your cue to rev the engine is when Shane says, 'That's him.'"

"Got it."

Gus turned to me. "Jessie, we don't need you for the blocking scene. You just sit tight until we shoot for real. There's no sense in you going through this twice."

"Okay," I agreed. I moved to the sidelines, watching

Shane. He was dressed in tight jeans and a black T-shirt, standing by the car, a souped-up red Mustang GT. If he was nervous, he covered it well, standing relaxed by the car, waiting for the action to begin. He caught me staring, and winked at me. I grinned back, happy that I was going to be in the car with him in a few minutes.

Gus gave some last-minute instructions to the rest of the "gang," who were supposed to come barreling out of the diner, jump on their Harleys, and take off down the highway. Tracy stood on the sidelines, snapping pictures. She was glad that her camera had resurfaced, and was happy to be back taking pictures.

After two more run-throughs, they finally decided it was time to do a take. "Ready to roll, darlin'?" Shane asked. I nodded and he gently brushed a wisp of hair off my cheek. "I like your hair that way. It shows off your beautiful face."

"Thanks." I gingerly stepped over lights and cables to slide into the front seat next to him.

A crew member held a light meter up to my face. "Once we get the cameras set up, you won't be able to open these doors, okay?" I nodded, and a production assistant named Sally handed me a little compact. "You can touch up your makeup if you want, but I think you look great."

"I don't want to ruin Arnie's work," I said, grinning at her. "I'll leave it alone. Does my hair look okay?"

"It's perfect," she said. "You were smart to wear it pulled

back. It won't be blowing all over your face once you pick up speed."

They set up cameras along the length of the Mustang on both sides, and Sy huddled with Lu Anne, discussing the shot. One camera was mounted on the front of the car and a pair were mounted on the sides, for close-ups of Shane and me.

"Take it nice and easy, everyone," Sy called out. I had expected fireworks after Lu Anne's dropping the bomb about the *StarGazer* article, but Sy was as calm as could be. *The calm before the storm?* I wondered.

"Feelin' a little nervous?" Shane was smiling at me, drumming his fingers impatiently on the steering wheel. He had a restless energy about him, and it seemed almost impossible for him to ever sit still.

"I've never done a high-speed chase before," I told him. "I'm just glad I'm not driving."

Shane was silent for a moment, watching as the extras and stuntmen on motorcycles moved into position. "That guy you introduced me to before," he said abruptly, "is he your boyfriend?"

My stomach did a little flip-flop. "Marc? Of course not. He lives in New Orleans."

Shane shot me a serious look. I loved his tawny dark eyes, so intense, so sexy. "I didn't ask where he lived, darlin'. I asked if he was your boyfriend."

I hesitated. I wanted to be truthful, but I didn't feel like talking about Marc. Somehow it felt dishonest, almost like a betrayal, to reveal anything about our relationship. And why was Shane asking anyway? I wondered. "We met last summer in New Orleans," I said slowly.

"You're probably wondering why I'm asking," Shane said, as if he could read my mind. When I didn't answer, he reached over and ran his fingers slowly down my bare arm, setting off a little zing of electricity along my nerve endings. "You know we've got something special goin', don't you, Jess?" He smiled a sexy, lopsided grin, and I felt myself melting. "I've never met anyone like you before." He brushed his long blond hair out of his eyes. "I came here to make a movie, and never expected I'd find someone like you. They say the best things happen when you're not even lookin' for them. I guess they're right."

"Maybe they are," I said softly. "Because I wasn't looking for anything either."

"So," he said, entwining his fingers around mine, "we're going to see where this takes us, right? I mean, I don't want this to end when the shoot is over, do you?"

"No," I gulped. "I don't want it to end, either." I hadn't thought that far ahead, but what would happen when the film company left town? Shane had his life in California and I had my life in Bedford. "You'll be going to back to L.A., though."

"That's why they've got planes," Shane said teasingly. "And the first thing we're gonna do is check the flights out of Bedford. I've got a million things I want to show you in Hollywood, Jess. Ever been out there?"

I shook my head. Outside of some trips to the ocean and that summer in New Orleans, I hardly ever left Bedford. "It seems like another planet," I admitted. "I can't even imagine what your life is like out there." I grinned. "Is it like that song from *The Beverly Hillbillies* . . . you know, where they talk about swimmin' pools and movie stars?"

Shane laughed, a deep throaty sound that made my pulse race. "Somethin' like that. I'm a pretty lucky guy, you know, because I'm going to show it to you. We'll go everywhere, Jessie. We'll start with Spago, they have the best pizza in town, and we'll drive up and down the Sunset Strip. That's really a trip, you won't believe some of the sights!"

"I've heard of the Sunset Strip," I told him. "I always wondered what it was like."

"Then we'll drive down to Venice and rent us some Rollerblades. I can't wait to show you the pier at Santa Monica. It's really cool; I love the ocean. We'll sit outside at one of those little places on the boardwalk and have dinner. I could sit there for hours, just watching all the people. Man, I don't know where to start." He eyed my floral sundress. "And there's great shopping on Rodeo Drive. Really famous designer stores. You've probably heard of all that." I nodded.

"And one of my favorite places is the planetarium at Griffith Park. You can see the Hollywood sign from the parking lot. We'll go there at sunset and you'll get a view of the whole city."

"But won't you be busy working? Making more movies?" I asked him.

"Sure, but you'll be with me, just like now," he said. "You'll get to see all the big studios and see how they operate. We'll be acting in movies together, Jessie. I told you we make a good team."

"It sounds wonderful," I said, just as Sandy blasted us with the bullhorn. The way Shane was talking, I'd have to spend a whole month out on the West Coast. Or maybe a whole summer. I smiled, thinking it all sounded like a dream. Would I really be going with him when he made movies? Was that really possible?

I glanced at Shane, tanned and drop-dead gorgeous, so sexy and confident. I relaxed a little, leaning back in the seat. I never would have believed it if someone had told me that I would be sitting here, right this minute, getting ready to film a scene with him.

Shane was a movie star, so maybe anything was possible. He could make magic, I was sure of it.

"Stand by!" Sandy shouted in the megaphone, nearly blasting my eardrum.

"Get ready to roll, Jess," Shane said. "And remember, darlin' . . . this is just the beginnin'."

Half an hour later, I couldn't wait for my short-lived career as a stunt girl to be over. Marc was right. I just wasn't cut out for this. My heart was in my throat the whole time Shane gunned the overheated engine like we were in the home stretch at the NASCAR races. Once we even made a ninety-degree turn on two tires. Shane's door almost touched the pavement as the car slid crazily down the highway on its side, and the acrid smell of burning rubber filled my lungs. I thought I would be physically sick as my heart pounded and my throat burned, but Shane had yelped with pure joy.

We had gone from zero to sixty in three seconds when Sy had yelled for action, and the next few minutes were a blur of high-speed chases, screeching starts and stops with gravel flying. Shane was a top-notch driver, but my stomach was doing cartwheels and I couldn't wait for the mad ride to be over. It reminded me of when I was six years old and went on Space Mountain after drinking a double frosted banana shake. The banana frosted had made an encore appearance all over my Winnie the Pooh T-shirt. I winced at the memory.

I was pale and shaky when we finally lurched to a stop, with the engine smoking and the car still rocking. I was amazed that I was in one piece, with no bumps or bruises. It seemed like a miracle.

"It's a wrap! Good job, everyone!" Sandy shouted and everyone cheered.

"Are you okay, Jess? You're lookin' a little pale," Shane said. He leaned over and gently undid my seat belt. "I think you need to get some air and move around a little, that's all. That's the best cure for motion sickness."

Motion sickness? I felt like I might never walk again. "Okay," I said, slipping out of the car. "You did a great job, Shane," I told him and he winked at me.

"I'll make sure my next movie doesn't have any car chases, Jessie."

"Your next movie?" I stepped out of the car, my knees rubbery, my skin clammy.

Shane grinned. "The one we're starring in together, darlin'."

I was going to star in his next movie? I felt like pinching myself, and then remembered something Shane had said. *Dreams do come true.*

I was headed to the trailer I shared with an actress named Jamie, when Maisie walked by, pushing a rack of dresses. "Hon, there's a message for you in the production office. I happened to see it sticking out of your mailbox."

"Oh, thanks," I said, glad my pulse rate had almost returned to normal. I stopped by the office and nearly bumped into Lu Anne, who was storming out.

"Just the person I want to see!" she thundered. Oh no, I

thought. First I have to endure Shane's death-defying car stunts, and now the Incredible Hulk! "Would you like to explain this?" She waved one of those little "While You Were Out" memos in my face. "This was in your box."

"If you give me a second to read it, maybe I can," I said, standing my ground and feeling good about it. I grabbed the memo and scanned it. "To Jessie Phillips from Rick Morgan. Please call me ASAP at 1-714-555-1212. We need to talk." I turned it over, puzzled.

"I don't get it—"

"Then let me explain it, sweetie," Lu Anne cut in nastily. "He probably wants to do a follow-up story with you. Here's a great story idea you can pitch to him. How about a story about a sweet little small-town chick who gets a big break in a Hollywood movie. Except it turns out she's not so sweet after all. She betrays the cast and crew for an easy buck, and ruins the whole film!" Lu Anne's face was flushed, her voice tight with rage. "Sound familiar, Jessie?"

"Lu Anne, I don't know what you're talking about!" I blurted out. I instinctively took a step backward, banging my thigh against a metal desk. "Who is this Rick Morgan? I've never heard of him."

"Oh, please." Lu Anne groaned. "You're telling me you don't remember Rick Morgan from *StarGazer?* He sure seems to remember you. I should have known you were the ungrateful little creep who leaked that story about Gus and the stuntmen. I suppose you got your little friend Tracy to give you the picture of Sandy sleeping under the tree, too. Wait till Sy hears about this," she said, her mouth stretching into a hard line. "You'll both be off the set so fast, your heads will spin."

"Lu Anne, I swear I don't know anything about this. I had never even heard of Rick Morgan until this morning, when I read his byline in that article. Look," I said, picking up the phone. "Call him right now, and see for yourself. Call Rick Morgan and that'll settle it." Out of the corner of my eye, I saw that everyone in the production office had stopped working to listen to our conversation. The room was very still. We were putting on quite a show, I thought grimly.

"That isn't necessary," Lu Anne blustered, but I saw a flicker of doubt cross her face. Maybe it finally dawned on her that I'd been framed. But by whom? Who really wanted me off the set?

"Lu Anne, use your head. Anyone could have put that note in my mailbox. They could have gotten the number of *StarGazer* from Information. Or maybe that's not the real number. There's one way to find out. Call this Rick Morgan. Right now. I insist." I sat on the edge of the desk, telling myself to remain calm. Lu Anne was a bully and if I backed down now, she'd win.

Without a word, Lu Anne picked up the phone and punched in some numbers. She turned her back to me, and

I could see Mavis, the receptionist, straining to listen. "Hi, is this Rick Morgan? Lu Anne Cobb here from Fearless Productions. I'm calling about a message you left for Jessie Phillips." Lu Anne glanced over her shoulder at me, her expression unreadable. "Jessie Phillips," she repeated slowly. "You left a message for her to call you. She's one of our cast members, and I'd like to know what it's all about." There was a long pause, and I heard Lu Anne sigh. "Okay, sorry about that. There must have been some mixup." Her voice hardened. "No, I don't have any comment about the story you ran on us. Anything we have to say will come through our publicity person. Thanks for your time."

Lu Anne put the phone down and turned to face me. "Well," she said, taking a deep breath, "it sounds pretty fishy to me, but Morgan said he never heard of you." She gave me a hard look. "He's been out of the office all morning and he swears he never called you."

I breathed a sigh of relief. "Lu Anne, I hate to say I told you so," I began.

"But you told me so," she said, flashing a rare smile. She shook her head. "I don't know what got into me, Jessie. That *StarGazer* article today was just the finishing touch. Between that and the dailies, I feel like everything's falling apart."

"What's wrong with the dailies?"

"You haven't heard? I thought word would have spread

around the set by now. Bad news usually travels fast. Two days' worth of dailies are messed up. They're grainy, completely unusable. All that film will have to be reshot. It wasn't anybody's fault, I guess it was just bad film. It sure makes things tough, though. We're already running over budget." She ran her hand through her choppy blond hair. "Like they say, when it rains, it pours."

Lu Anne hurried away to take a call, and I decided to grab a soda from the canteen. The dinner buffet wasn't set up yet, but I knew they always kept extra sodas in a tub of ice in a little equipment shed back by the tennis courts.

I was almost at the shed, when Tracy came dashing across the lawn, a funny look on her face. "Jess," she said breathlessly. She took in my wrinkled sundress and wild hair. The French braid hadn't held up as well as I had hoped, and there were limp strands hanging around my face. "How'd the chase scene go? I want to hear all about it! Don't you want to get cleaned up for dinner?" She seemed jittery as she grabbed my elbow and tried to steer me away from the shed.

"No, I want to get a cold drink first." I shook her hand off my arm and wiggled past her. "I can practically taste the dust from that chase scene. I'll tell you all about it after I get a soda."

"Oh, don't bother having a soda now. You can have one with dinner," she said brightly. "Or iced tea, wouldn't that be nice? I know they'll have iced tea with dinner." She slung her arm around my shoulder, trying to pull me along with her.

I stared at her. "Tracy, what's wrong with you? Dinner isn't for another couple of hours. I can't wait that long. I'm parched, I feel like my mouth is packed with cotton."

"I'll get you a soda, Jess. I'll bring it to your trailer," she said a little wildly. "Just tell me what you want and I'll get it—honest!"

"I want a soda, Tracy, and I want it now." I reached past her to pull open the door to the shed.

"Wait!" she said, blocking my path.

"Now what?" I was running out of patience with Tracy's jabbering.

"There aren't any sodas left, I meant to tell you," she said, the words tumbling out over each other in a mad rush. "They're all gone."

"What are you talking about? I just saw some extras drinking sodas."

"Well, they might have sodas, but there's no ice, so they're drinking warm sodas. That's it, they're out of ice," she said quickly.

I nearly laughed in her face. Tracy is the worst liar on the planet. "Tracy, are you nuts? The heat must have gotten to you because I think you're delusional. Now let go of me."

I flung her arm off, reached out for the door handle, and suddenly stopped, a sick feeling washing over me. I heard laughter coming from the shed. Male laughter, low and sexy, that could only belong to Shane Rockett. My antennae went up. I held my breath, my heart doing a drumbeat in my chest. Shane was alone in the shed, laughing? That didn't make any sense.

Except he wasn't alone. I heard a feminine, musical little laugh that was the trademark of someone I knew very well: Heidi Hopkins. It was ninety degrees out and Shane and Heidi were laughing together in the shed with the door closed. I didn't have to be a rocket scientist to figure out what was going on.

But there was only way to know for sure.

I looked at Tracy. "Is that who I think it is?"

She nodded, a stricken look on her face. "Shane and Heidi," she whispered. "They've been in there for a while. Please, Jessie, let's just go away and try to forget about it."

"Go away? No way!"

I yanked open the door to the shed with such force, I nearly tumbled backward when it suddenly gave way. I could feel the blood drain from my face, and a wave of dizziness washed over me when I saw Shane and Heidi locked in a hot embrace. Shane glanced up with a deer-in-the-headlights expression before he jumped away from Heidi.

Heidi was staring at me with a funny half-smile plastered on her face, and I wondered for one crazy moment if this was part of a plan—that maybe she wanted me to discover them.

But she was my friend, wasn't she? Nothing made sense anymore.

I couldn't take my eyes off Shane. Once the initial shock of seeing me was over, he made a fast recovery and cranked up the down-home charm, ambling toward me with outstretched arms.

"Jessie, darlin'," he said, wiping his brow. "I was just going to get you a soda. I bet you worked up a thirst after that wild ride." He stopped to reach into the tub of icy drinks and pulled out a cola. "How's this one—"

I turned on my heel and grabbed Tracy, who was staring at us slack-jawed in shock. "C'mon, Tracy, let's get out of here."

"Hey, Jess," Shane yelled after me, "don't you want a soda?" I didn't turn my head, but I heard Heidi's soft voice murmuring to him. He sprinted after me and tugged at my hand. "Jess, you've gotta believe me. This isn't what it looks like—"

I snorted and wheeled around to face him. "Oh, puhleeze! It's exactly what it looks like, you two-timing creep!" He reached for me again, but I yanked my hand away as hot tears stung my eyes. I headed for my trailer at a near-gallop, with Tracy bringing up the rear. I didn't stop running until I got inside and slammed the door. I threw myself on the cheap daybed, my heart pounding, and tried to push down the throat-clogging emotion that threatened to overwhelm me.

Like the song says, I had been a fool for love. Big-time.

"Jess, I'm really sorry you had to see that," Tracy said softly. She handed me a tissue and sat on a folding chair across from me. "Don't be upset, he's not worth it."

"You're right," I told her, yanking the rubber band out of my hair. "He is *so* not worth it." A wall of limp, sticky hair fell on my neck as the French braid came undone. I suddenly remembered there was someone I needed to talk to. "Tracy," I said, "do you have your cell phone with you?"

"Sure." She dug into her backpack and handed it to me.

"There's something I have to do." I dialed information with trembling fingers and got the number for the Bedford Airport. Would I be too late? I glanced at my watch. Marc's plane had probably already left, but I had to check anyway. There were so many things I wanted to say to him! I felt a stab of guilt, remembering that I had been so wrapped up with Shane, I had practically ignored Marc during his visit. Maybe it wasn't too late to make amends.

A minute later, I was connected with a gate agent who told me Marc's plane had just taken off. I shook my head and handed the phone back to Tracy, who nodded sympathetically. "What do we do now?" she said. I heard some muffled shouts and movement outside the trailer and wondered if the catering staff was already setting up the buffet.

"I don't want to see Shane again today," I said hurriedly. "Or Heidi. Let's zip out of here before they start serving dinner. We can grab a pizza at Sal's and go back to my place." I splashed some water on my face and ran a brush through my tangled hair. "Just peek outside to make sure the coast is clear."

Chapter Twelve

⭐

"YOU GOT IT," TRACY SAID, JUMPING UP. SHE OPENED THE DOOR a crack and her eyes widened. "What in the—" she began. A wailing siren drowned out the rest of the sentence. "Yikes, what's going on? Jess, look—there's an ambulance and a fire truck coming up the driveway."

"Everybody out! Fire on the set!" Somebody thumped the side of the trailer and I saw Lu Anne running toward one of the big trailers parked under the elms. They were the big Gulfstreams, reserved for the stars and major players. Gus was already there, trying to chop through the metal door with a crowbar, while curls of smoke drifted out from underneath the trailer. We dashed over and stood at the edge of the crowd, watching as Sy and Lu Anne urged Gus to hurry. Was someone trapped inside?

"It's Crystal's trailer," Tracy said. "I wonder what could have happened?"

"She was probably smoking in bed again," Julie said, rolling her eyes. "This has happened a couple of times before, you know. I don't know why they even bothered calling the fire department. Now they'll probably be late serving dinner."

Tracy and I exchanged a look. It was obvious Crystal wasn't very popular with her fellow crew members. The fire company took over then, crashing through the trailer door with a battering ram and dashing inside with long, coiling hoses.

A moment later, Crystal emerged, looking as limp as a noodle, being supported by two brawny firemen. They helped Crystal out of the trailer, then turned her over to the paramedics, who slapped an oxygen mask on her face and a blood pressure cuff on her arm. Two firemen tossed a charred sofa on the tarmac and began hosing it down, moving back as swirls of gray smoke rose from the cushions. Crystal sat on a blanket on the grass, looking pale and dazed, as both Sy and Lu Anne squatted down to talk to her, speaking in low tones. Sy was holding her hand, waving away the bystanders crowded around her. "Move back! She needs air!" he shouted.

"Do you think it's serious?" Tracy asked.

"Nah," Julie said in a bored voice. "But this should be a good lesson to everyone. This is why Sy doesn't allow smoking on the set. We don't have the insurance coverage for one thing, and it's just crazy to take a risk like this. He should have gotten rid of Crystal years ago. I don't know why he keeps her around."

"It may not be her fault," Chad Stevens said. "Those sofas catch on fire easily. Even a tiny spark will set off a blaze. It's something about the finishing they use on the material." He looked around the crowd, probably searching for Heidi. She had given him the cold shoulder ever since that night he had tried to eat dinner with us, but he refused to take the hint, still following her around like a lost puppy.

"She'll be fine, folks," I heard Gus say. He wiped his hands on his pants and moved toward a little knot of crew members.

"See, what did I tell you?" Julie sounded disappointed. "She was probably watching the afternoon soaps and smoking in bed. She does that a lot when she's not scheduled to be in a scene."

Gus joined us then, shaking his head. "Can't believe she had that trailer door locked," he said. "She must have passed out from the smoke, and there was no way for her to get out. What was she thinking?"

"You're a real hero," Julie said, smirking a little. "No one else would have gone in after her."

Lu Anne walked over, pushing everyone back. "Show's over, folks. They're gonna take her to the hospital, but it's just for observation. The fire marshal would like to clear the area so he can do his job. How about everyone heading over to the dining area? We're going to serve dinner early tonight. Barbecued beef and lemon pie."

"This is our cue to leave," I whispered to Tracy. I spotted Shane at the edge of the crowd, and I wanted to make a quick getaway before we made eye contact.

"Tracy? I need to talk to you!" Tracy jumped as Sy's voice rang out. She raised her eyebrows in a questioning look and I nudged her back toward the fire scene.

"Go ahead, I'll wait for you at the circle." I glanced nervously toward Shane. He still hadn't spotted me, and was walking toward the buffet setup.

"Okay. Catch you then."

"YOU'RE NOT GOING TO BELIEVE THIS," TRACY SAID TEN minutes later. We were walking home from the set. It was a beautiful early-summer night in Bedford; the air was warm and sultry, softened by a gentle breeze off the river.

"Try me." We stepped into Sal's and placed an order for

two large pizzas, one veggie and one pepperoni. I hadn't quite converted Tracy to vegetarianism yet, but I was working on it.

"Sy took my camera," she said flatly. "He said they may need it as evidence."

"Are you kidding me?" I was stunned. "Evidence for what?"

Tracy lowered her voice as if the guy behind the counter whirling pizza dough would broadcast her news to the world. "The fire marshal said he's suspicious about the blaze in Crystal's trailer. They didn't say anything at the scene, because they didn't want to tip off anyone. He thinks it may be arson, but he can't be sure until he does a complete investigation. They're going to take the sofa with them on the truck. It had a funny smell, like someone had poured a strong chemical on it."

"Arson? How could that be? Julie said that Crystal likes to smoke in bed and that she's done this before. It seems like a stretch. Besides who would want to hurt Crystal?" Tracy rolled her eyes, and I quickly backpedaled. "Okay, she's not the most popular person in the world, but I don't think anyone on the set would want to turn her into a human barbecue."

"You never know," Tracy said mysteriously. "Sy swore me to secrecy, incidentally."

"I already figured that out. I'm not going to say a word to anyone, believe me." We paid for the pizzas and headed down Main Street toward my house. "I still don't see what your camera has to do with anything. Sy doesn't think you were involved with the fire, does he?"

"No, but he said I may have taken some shots that would be helpful to the investigation. I guess he wanted me to give him the camera so he could download everything himself. Or maybe even give it to the police, I'm not sure."

"What kind of shots?" The rich tomato smell of the pizza was wafting up from the cardboard box, making me realize how hungry I was. I hadn't eaten anything since early morning, and the chase scene with Shane hadn't done much for my appetite. And I had felt like the bottom dropped out of my stomach when I interrupted the romantic scene between Shane and Heidi in the shed.

"I took some atmosphere shots the other day, you know, just general shots of the set. It was sort of interesting to see the old ivy-covered buildings of Fairmont and the lake, with all the movie equipment set up, and the crew members milling around. Sy happened to walk by and looked through the viewfinder. He's interested in still photography and he said it was a good shot."

"I remember that shot. You got the edge of the lake and the extras feeding the Canada geese."

"Exactly. We were surprised they were still hanging around the pond, and that all the noise and commotion hadn't frightened them away."

Mom was working late, so Tracy and I reheated the pizza as soon as we got home. We were perched on high stools at the breakfast bar, munching contentedly, trying to figure out the arson—if that's what it really was.

"You know, Jessie," Tracy said, "if this was an episode of *CSI* there'd already be a few suspects by now. One or two would be really obvious, and one would be a wild card, someone you would never think of."

"You're right." I reached for another piece of pizza. "Okay, I'll play along. Let's take turns naming suspects and see what we come up with. I'll go first." I paused dramatically. "Gus Bartley, for starters. He and Crystal argued the other day. In fact, they argue every day."

"That's a good guess, but you're forgetting something. Gus is the one who tried to chop the door down to rescue her."

"I thought of that, but that could just be grandstanding. In fact, it's exactly the kind of thing you would do to throw somebody off the trail. I thought it was interesting that he was pounding away at the door with a crowbar, but the fire trucks were already steaming up the drive." I poured sodas for both of us. "Maybe it was all an act. Your turn."

"Heidi Hopkins."

I tried not to flinch at the name. "Because?"

"Crystal said awful things about her acting and said she never wants to work with her again."

I shook my head. "I'm no fan of Heidi's, but I don't think she has much of a motive. Heidi is a big star, and Crystal is a has-been. No one's really going to care what Crystal thinks when it comes to a casting decision. Sy definitely wouldn't."

"So that's it, then? Just two suspects?"

"Maybe Shane? No, scratch that. It's probably too crazy."

"Why Shane? He always kids around with Crystal. From what I've seen the two of them get along together pretty well."

"Yes, but Crystal has a nasty tongue. She was making jokes about his method acting the other day, and I remember how annoyed he looked. Maybe that country-boy charm is hiding a big temper."

"Being annoyed isn't enough of a reason to fry someone. You'd have to have a grudge against them. Something really important. Maybe something that went back a long way."

"You might be right," I told Tracy. "Then we're back to square one—Gus. You know, I always had the funny idea that they had some kind of a history together. Crystal made some snide remarks to him about money. She hinted that he would do anything for a buck."

"Well, we're not going to settle this tonight," Tracy said. She checked her watch and jumped down. "I have to scoot and you have a call to make."

It was nearly ten when I caught up with Marc. His voice, low and sexy, raced over the wires and I felt a tug at my heart.

How had I let him get away without telling him how much he meant to me?

"It's good to hear from you, Jess. I miss you already. I was just going to call you."

"I miss you, too," I told him. *More than you can imagine.* "I wish you could have been here this afternoon. The place was hopping." I told him about the fire in Crystal's trailer and the drama on the set. I even told him about Sy taking Tracy's camera for the investigation and he whistled softly in surprise.

"As long as you weren't hurt, *cher*," he said in that thrilling, sexy voice. "You're still planning on coming down here at the end of summer, right?"

"I'm counting on it," I assured him. "It will give me something to look forward to."

"Me too." I hung up, thinking for the first time that I would be glad when the film shoot was over and the movie company would leave Bedford. Suddenly, I didn't care anymore about *Reckless Summer*, my short-lived career as a movie actress, or the chance to go to Beverly Hills and hang out with celebrities. Hollywood had lost all its appeal for me.

All I really wanted was waiting for me in New Orleans.

AT SIX-THIRTY THE NEXT MORNING, TRACY AND I WERE HUD-dled together, munching on donuts, checking the call-in sheet under a cloudy sky. I was relieved to see that I didn't have any scenes with Shane that day, and I wondered how he would react when we finally were thrown together again.

"Nothing with you and Shane together," Tracy said, reading my mind. "That's a break."

I nodded. "Not so lucky with Heidi, though." I was scheduled for a group scene with Heidi in the late afternoon, but with any luck, I could keep my distance until then.

And then Julie, the production assistant, dropped a bombshell.

"Have you heard the news?" Julie asked, her brown eyes snapping with excitement. "Chad Stevens confessed! He told the cops he set the fire in Crystal's trailer. So it wasn't an accident after all."

"What? I don't believe it," Tracy said, shaking her head in disbelief. She bent down to fumble with the settings on a new camera that Sy had let her borrow for the rest of the shoot. "Chad always seemed like Mr. Nice Guy. Did he say why he did it?"

"Nobody knows. I didn't even know that he knew Crystal. I think this is the first time he's ever worked with her. No one knows much about him," she said thoughtfully. "I've heard he has a major crush on Heidi, but that's all. He pretty much keeps to himself."

Lu Anne approached, clipboard in hand, cell phone attached to her ear. She snapped the phone shut with a decisive snap and shot a keen look at us, her mouth tense. "I can see you've already heard about Chad. Good, that will save me a lot of unnecessary explanations." She immediately began riffling through her papers, as if to ward off any unwelcome questions.

"None of us can believe it," Tracy insisted. "Why did he do it? Does anybody know?"

Lu Anne pinned Tracy with an irritated look and started handing out new pages of dialogue. "I have no idea," she said tightly. "That's something for the police to figure out. I just want to say one thing, and then I'm not going to mention this again. I expect everyone to be really professional and not breathe a word of this to any outsiders." She glanced at Tracy, a questioning look in her eyes. I wondered if Lu Anne still had doubts about my and Tracy's loyalty, even after her chat with Rick Morgan from *StarGazer*.

"I'm not going to say a word about this!" Tracy retorted, on the defensive. "No one's going to get one syllable out of me."

"Okay, but I'm just warning you. There might be some reporters from the Bedford paper here today. They may try to talk to all of you," she added, sweeping us with her intense gaze, "and they might be pretty aggressive about it, so I want you all to remember something: If anyone asks you about the fire—or about anything else—the only acceptable response is 'no comment.' You got that?"

She waited until we nodded before pointing to the wooden sawhorses that were set up at the edge of the winding drive. "Sy hired some extra security people today, so they should keep be able to keep the press away."

"So these are today's new sides?" I asked her.

"That's right. You've got some new dialogue to learn, because we've cut Chad's part out of the picture. He had a small role, so it shouldn't be any real problem." She stared at the gray sky filled with threatening clouds and turned up the collar on her jeans jacket. "They're predicting showers this afternoon, so we may have to close down production early. That's all, gang."

Her cell phone rang then, and she wrenched it out of her pocket just as a roll of thunder cracked in the distance. Lu Anne barked a few clipped words into the phone and then took off at a loping trot across the lawn.

"Wow, I still can't believe it," Tracy said. "Chad Stevens is the last person I would have suspected. He always seemed so friendly and polite."

Gus wandered over then, looking more grizzled and rumpled than usual. "Funny about that young feller Chad, isn't it?" he said, helping himself to two jelly donuts and a sugary bear claw. Gus obviously wasn't into Atkins. "It's the quiet ones you have to watch out for, you know. Still waters run deep and all that. It just goes to show you never know about people." He grabbed three sugar packets for his coffee and sighed happily. "Maybe now things can get back to normal around here."

"So what do you think?" I asked Tracy after Gus drifted away. "So much for our detective skills. Chad wasn't even on our suspect list."

Tracy shook her head. "I know. We were way off base. I wish I knew why he did it, though. There's just something about it that doesn't seem right. Where's the motive?"

"I can't even guess." I hesitated. "But he had the knowledge to do it. Remember somebody said Chad knew a lot about pyrotechnics? And when the fireman threw the sofa on the grass, Chad said that maybe it had a flammable finish on it and that's what started the fire. Why would he say that? Didn't you think that was a little odd?"

"Now I do." Tracy shrugged. "I didn't think too much about it at the time." She paused, fingering the new camera. "Well, it's over, I guess, since he confessed. I can turn this in and get my own camera back."

"It's not over yet, sweetie!" I recognized the rasping voice of Crystal Hall before I turned around. "Be an angel, and get me a coffee," she said to Tracy. "I've got to sit down before I fall down," she said, suddenly slumping onto a folding chair. "Put lots of real sugar into it, hon, not that fake stuff. And a donut, too. I need some quick energy. I'm as shaky as a leaf."

"Crystal, what are you doing here?" I asked in surprise. "We thought you were still in the hospital."

"Nah," she said, waving her hand dismissively. "The docs insisted on keeping me for observation, even though I told them there wasn't a thing in the world wrong with me. They finally let me out late last night." She nodded as Tracy handed her a paper cup of coffee. "Thanks, doll."

"Are you sure you should be working today? You looked really sick after the fire." I flashed on a vision of Crystal looking pale and drawn, with an oxygen mask strapped to her face.

"Oh, I'm a tough old bird, you know," Crystal said, her green eyes flashing. "It will take more than Gus Bartley to do me in." She grabbed a lemon donut and bit into it with relish. "Hah—wait till he sees me on the set today, big as life. That will fix his wagon!"

"Gus?" Tracy and I exchanged a look. "What does he have to do with this?"

Crystal glanced over her shoulder, as if she were afraid of being overheard. "Gus has everything to do with it," she said smugly. She paused for dramatic effect, as little puffs of steam from the hot coffee swirled around her lined face. "I'll let you know a little secret. Gus is the one who set the fire. He's the one the police should be after."

I stared at her while she sipped her coffee, her sharp eyes

roaming over the set. "Gus? But haven't you heard the news? Chad confessed to everything. I think he's already in police custody."

"I heard," Crystal said grimly. "And I don't know what that boy was thinking of, confessing to something he didn't do. Somebody must have pressured him into it. Why, that boy wouldn't hurt a fly."

Tracy and I exchanged a look. "That's exactly what we thought," Tracy said quietly. "Crystal, I know you and Gus aren't crazy about each other, but do you really think he would do anything to hurt you?"

"Hah! I know he would, that old buzzard." Crystal patted the pocket of her cotton sweater and frowned. "Out of cigarettes again," she muttered. "I must have left them at the hospital."

"But why?" I blurted out. "Why would Gus want to hurt you?"

Crystal shot me a shrewd look. "There's a lot you don't know, sweetie," she said smoothly. "Let's just say that Gus would like me out of the picture, for good." She sipped the coffee and made a face. "He hoped that everybody would think I was responsible for the fire, smoking in bed, you know. Sy had that written into my contract." She shook her head. "No smoking in the trailer, or Sy could fire me on the spot. Of course, the contract wouldn't matter, because if

Gus had his way, I'd be incinerated by now anyway!" She gave a harsh laugh and wiped her lips.

"What are you going to do?" I saw that they were setting up the first shot, and I wanted to get to my trailer before Shane spotted me.

"I'm going to tell the authorities," Crystal said simply. "I know Gus did it, and it's up to them to prove it. Unless they're complete idiots, they'll let that poor boy out of jail and arrest the right person. But first I'm going to give Gus a piece of my mind. I can't wait to see the look on his face." She stood up unsteadily and then suddenly doubled over, her body wracked with a series of deep, hacking coughs.

"Can I get you anything?" Tracy jumped up, alarmed.

"Just one more favor, hon," Crystal said, thumping her chest with her bony hand. "Check to see if that doctor called in a prescription for me. They were going to leave it in my new trailer. It's that shiny silver one there," she said, pointing to the edge of the lot. "All that smoke I took in," she said apologetically, "it makes it hard to walk. It will be sitting right on the counter."

"I'll get it for you, Crystal, don't worry about a thing," Tracy said. "Catch you later, Jess."

Chapter Thirteen

⭐

"HELLO, DARLIN'," A FAMILIAR LOW VOICE SAID BEHIND ME AS I headed for my trailer a few minutes later.

Shane. In the flesh. Looking tan and wildly sexy in skintight Diesels that molded his hips and thighs, showing off his buff body. He was enough to set any female's pulse fluttering within a hundred yards. Except the thrill was gone for me, as the song says. Or was it?

"Hi, Shane," I said, hoping my voice wouldn't quaver. My traitorous heart went into overdrive just being near him, but I willed myself to play it cool. *Be just as casual as he is,* I warned myself.

"Need some company?" he said, strolling along beside me. "Looks like we might get some rain today," he added, squinting at the dark sky and roiling thunderclouds. "Lu Anne will have a fit. She and Sy want to wrap up a few key scenes today. All that mess with Chad slowed things down, you know." He paused, finally noticing that I wasn't saying a word. He reached over and tapped playfully on my bare arm. "So, what do you think about all that? Bet you didn't imagine old Chad would turn out like that, did you?" He shook his head in amazement, and then looked up at me under dark, sooty lashes.

"Pretty unbelievable," I said tightly.

He relaxed a little, deciding that I was going to talk to him after all. Did he think I was going to let the scene with Heidi in the shed vanish from my memory banks? As Crystal would say, *Dream on, buster!*

"It sure is," he said readily. "I was just sayin' to Gus that I didn't know he had it in him. It's not like Crystal every did anythin' to him."

"No, I'm sure she didn't," I said flatly. We were almost at my trailer, and I wondered, for one crazy moment, if Shane thought I was going to invite him in.

"You know, Jess," he said seriously, "with everything that's been happenin', I'm thinking they may wrap this shoot early. At least the Bedford part of it."

"Do you think so?" I replied with zero interest.

"I do," he said, nodding his head up and down. "First that article in *StarGazer*, and then those dailies getting messed up. And now this trouble with Chad. I think Sy figures the sooner we pull out of town, the better."

"Maybe he's right," I said carefully. "Maybe it would be best if everyone just . . . cleared out . . . as quickly as possible."

Shane's blue eyes clouded, and I realized the deep-freeze treatment had finally penetrated his brain. "Well, you know, Jess," he said, reaching for my hand, "this isn't the end of things for us." He moved close to me, and I could smell his clean male scent mixed with a whiff of lemon aftershave.

"Isn't it?"

"Why of course not," Shane said stammering a little. Two giggling extras wandered by and checked him out. "You don't think . . . uh, Jess . . . what you saw in the shed . . . that didn't mean anything, you know."

I waited. He leaned over and traced his fingertips down my bare arm. "We still have a couple of weeks left here, and then we have Hollywood. That's all ahead of us, Jess. It's just sitting there, waiting for you and me," he said, stretching his arms out expansively. "Paradise, that's what it is, Jess. Paradise."

I stared at him with new eyes, new understanding. He suddenly seemed like an actor playing a role, with his carefully modulated voice and practiced gestures.

"Really?" I stared at him coolly.

"Just a word from you, and it can all happen," he added, his tawny dark eyes searching mine.

And then the most amazing thing happened. I laughed. A happy laugh that billowed up from deep inside me and burst through my lips. "I have a word for you, Shane," I said, nearly giddy with relief that the Shane spell was broken. "Are you listening carefully?" I waited till he nodded, and then leaned close, enjoying the feeling of the word on my tongue. "Good-bye!" I said with a big smile.

"What are you talking about?" he blustered. A muscle ticked in his chiseled jaw. The look on his face was priceless.

"That's the magic word. Good-bye." I repeated it, savoring the moment.

"Jess, what's gotten into you? I don't understand . . ." Shane began, but it didn't matter because I was already tugging open the trailer door.

I smiled at him again, suddenly feeling lighter than I had in weeks. "Good-bye Shane," I repeated, rolling the word around in my mouth. Who would have thought that one word could have sounded so delicious to my own ears? "Good-bye, good-bye, good-bye."

I saw Shane's eyes first widen in amazement, and then narrow to an angry squint as I shut the trailer door in his face. *Poor Shane*, I thought, breathing a big sigh of relief. He obviously wasn't used to taking no for an answer!

* * *

I CAUGHT UP WITH TRACY LATER THAT MORNING ON THE WAY
to the production office. "You're not going to believe this,"
she said, tugging at my arm. "I found out something about
Gus and Crystal. You were right, they do have a history together, and that's why Crystal thinks he set the fire."

I stopped dead in my tracks, more convinced than ever
that Chad was innocent. "What did you find out?"

"Do you remember when Crystal sent me to her trailer
to get her prescription?" Tracy paused, looking a little embarrassed. "I did something that maybe I shouldn't have . . ."
Her voice trailed off uncertainly, and she stared at her
shoes, her face flushing. "I mean, technically, it was like
snooping, but when you think about it—"

"Tracy, out with it!" A light rain was falling and we
ducked under a canopy near the tennis courts. "What happened in the trailer? What did you do?"

"The pills weren't on the counter, and when I looked
around the trailer, I noticed the message light flashing on
her answering machine. I figured maybe it was the drugstore calling, so I decided to play the message." She bit her
lower lip, waiting for me to say something, but I made a gesture for her to continue. "There was a message all right. But
it wasn't from the drugstore . . . it was from Gus. And he
was steaming!"

"What about?" I kept my voice neutral as a couple of cameramen walked by, holding their light meters up toward the murky sky, checking out the next shot.

"He said he knew Crystal was spreading rumors that he was responsible for the fire, and that she better stop it right away." Tracy leaned close and said breathlessly, "but here's the part that really surprised me. He said, 'You know I've got the goods on you, and I can spill the beans whenever I want. So keep your trap shut.'"

"Wow," I said softly. *Keep your trap shut?* It sounds like Gus wasn't Mr. Warmth after all. "He's got the goods on her? What does that mean?"

Tracy shook her head. "I have no idea. But it sounds like he's trying to keep her from talking to the cops. So maybe Chad Stevens won't get out of jail after all." She pulled her sweater around her as a light rain started to fall. "The funny thing is, I really don't think Gus did it, and I don't think Chad did it. But I don't know where that leaves us."

We started walking back to the production office together, lost in thought. That leaves us empty-handed, I decided. Except something was nagging at the back of my mind. What was I missing?

Production ground to a halt when a torrential rain started right after lunch. Tracy and I had retrieved her camera from the production office and had gone back to my house to download the pictures of the cast and crew. We were sitting in my room, going over some "atmosphere shots" Tracy had taken, when I noticed something strange about one of the pictures.

"Tracy," I said slowly, "these shots are all taken in sequence, right? And you can tell by the numbers when they were taken?"

She nodded, admiring a shot of a spectacular sunset that she had printed out. "Right, there's a record of every single shot. They've all got the date and time marked on them. Why do you want to know?" she said absently.

"Well, this is really crazy, but look at this picture of the set you took last week. Check out the date and the time."

Tracy leaned over, her brow furrowed in concentration. "Something's wrong here," she said slowly. "This looks like the shot I took, but the timestamp on the bottom says it was taken yesterday morning." She lifted her gaze to mine, shaking her head. "I didn't even have the camera yesterday morning—it was in the production office."

Suddenly the pieces were starting to fit into place. "Tracy, someone else took this picture, don't you get it? Look at it carefully, what do you see?"

"It's just a picture of the set with the cameras and equipment," she said slowly. "Look, there's the pond in the background . . . and the trailers." She shrugged and passed the picture back to me. "There's nothing special about it—"

"Check out the pond," I interrupted her.

"What are you getting at?"

"The pond is empty," I said excitedly. "So where are the geese? Don't you remember? There were geese in the shot you took. We were surprised they were still hanging around Bedford and figured they would have flown back home by now. There should be geese in the shot, Tracy! Canada geese."

"Ohmigosh," she breathed softly. "You're right, Jess." Her breath hitched in her throat. "This looks a lot like the shot I took, but it's definitely not my shot. The geese are missing." Her fingers flew over the computer keys, her expression intent. "Somebody tried to make a duplicate shot. But why?" she muttered. "That's what we've got to find out."

"What are you doing?"

"I'm going to check the Recycle Bin. Remember how we couldn't download all the pictures because the battery was running low? Maybe the original picture—my picture—is in there. If I can pull up the original picture, we'll have proof someone's trying to pull a fast one."

A few minutes later, the truth was staring us in the face. Tracy's shot—the original shot she took with the geese in the background—was up on the screen. We compared it with the "new" version, and that's when it hit us.

"Jess, look at the trailer," Tracy said, pointing to a corner of the original photo.

I stared at the shiny silver edge of one of the stars' trailers. "It's Crystal's," I said. "There's the wind chime she keeps by the door. She says it's for good luck."

Tracy nodded. "It's Crystal's trailer, all right, but take a look at the front step. See that square thing lying there. I recognize it, do you?"

I squinted hard and made out the edges of a clipboard with some papers billowing in the breeze. "Looks like someone forgot their clipboard—" I began and clapped my hand over my mouth. "It's Lu Anne's clipboard," I said, as the truth suddenly dawned on me. "She must have forgotten it outside on the step when she went into Crystal's trailer. And the curtain on the trailer is open a little, you can see someone peering out." A hazy face was just visible behind the plaid curtain over the bay window.

"Probably Lu Anne," Tracy said. "She ducked inside Crystal's trailer to set things up for the fire, and then maybe she saw us taking pictures. She knew we'd spot the clipboard on the step, so she stole the camera to take another shot." Tracy paused. "Of course, now we've got to prove Lu Anne is the one who stole the camera and took the new picture."

"That's not going to be easy," I said. "I heard the police dusted the camera for fingerprints, and they couldn't find any."

"But I bet they didn't check the battery," Tracy said slowly. "They wouldn't have any reason to." She turned to me, her eyes flashing with excitement. "Jessie, the battery is the key, I just know it. If Lu Anne forgot and left her prints on the battery, then she'll have a lot of explaining to do."

"The battery was running low last week," I said. "I remember you said the red light kept coming on when you were trying to take some shots."

"And now it's fine." Tracy snapped the camera back into the case. "So somebody must have changed the battery, and that somebody has got to be Lu Anne!"

"YOU REALIZE WE ALREADY HAVE A SUSPECT IN CUSTODY?" Detective Pete Aldrich said later that afternoon.

"And the suspect has already confessed to arson?" his partner, Detective Mike Simmons, piped up.

"I know that," I said. I took a deep breath. "But it's all a mistake. I don't know why Chad Stevens confessed to setting that fire, but he didn't do it. I told you on the phone that we have new evidence, and here it is." I nodded to Tracy and she handed over her digital camera along with a folder full of prints.

"Oh, new evidence," Detective Aldrich said, rolling his eyes at his partner. "Well, that certainly changes the picture. We might as well take a look, now that you've come all the way down here." It was hard not to be put off by his condescending tone, but I didn't dare antagonize him. It had taken three phone calls, but the two detectives had finally agreed to meet with us at the Bedford police station at the end of Main Street.

Tracy and I were sitting across a battered metal desk from the two men, with the digital camera and some prints spread out in front of us. The square, dingy room was painted institutional green, and cigarette butts lined the grimy beige linoleum floor. I felt like I was caught up in an episode of *Law and Order*.

"You took these?" Detective Simmons raised his eyebrows at Tracy.

"Yes, as part of my video diary. It's for a school project," she explained patiently, even though I was sure the police already had all this information.

"We already dusted the camera for prints," the older detective, Detective Aldrich, said helpfully. "Nothing. I wasn't even sure why they even bothered. There's nothing on there that shows the fire."

"No, but there's plenty of incriminating information on here," Tracy said tightly.

"Okay, tell me about it." Detective Aldrich stared at her from under dark, bushy eyebrows. "What do you think we missed?"

"You didn't miss anything," Tracy said quickly, "it's just that you didn't know what to look for."

"And you do." His partner reached behind him to pour half a cup of murky coffee.

Tracy nodded. "Let me show you . . ."

Half an hour later, a red-faced Detective Aldrich opened the door of the interview room and walked us past the booking room to the front desk. His partner was still sitting at the metal desk, mulling over the shots, making notes on a legal pad. The detectives had said they would present the information to their supervisor, and then the D.A. When we got to the double glass doors leading to Main Street, his leathery face broke into a smile. "You girls did a good job. Excellent police work," he said, pumping our hands. "You found something we totally missed. This is all off the record, of course."

"Of course." I smiled at him. "When do you think you can wrap this up?"

"I think things will go fast once the D.A. sees this. And we'll dust the battery for prints, like you suggested. We still don't have a motive, but maybe that will come. Right now, we've got means and opportunity." He hesitated, seeming a little ill at ease. "I know it will be really tempting to talk about all this, but you girls know that everything we discussed today is confidential, don't you?"

"Of course." Tracy and I said in unison. "The one thing we've learned is how to keep a secret," she added with a wry smile.

*   *   *

BACK AT MY HOUSE, I WAS TOSSING A CAESAR SALAD FOR DIN-
ner when the phone rang. I reached over some plump garden tomatoes to take the call, and was surprised when
Shane's sexy voice raced across the line. I hopped up on a
bar stool, tucking the phone under my chin.

"I missed you at dinner," he said, without bothering to
identify himself. "What's up, darlin'?" It's funny but that low
husky voice didn't make my heart go *zing* this time. I continued to toss the salad, throwing in some freshly grated
parmesan. Mom raised her eyes questioningly, nodding at
the phone, but I just smiled.

"Well, they canceled the afternoon shooting because of
the rain, so there didn't seem to be any reason to hang
around."

"No reason?" He put on a mock-hurt voice. "What about
me?"

I laughed at Shane's enormous self-absorption, his Texas-
sized ego. Why hadn't I noticed it before? I had been blinded
by the sultry voice, the bedroom eyes, the whole sexy pack-
age. "Well, Shane," I said in a friendly tone, "what *about* you?"

A moment's pause while he recovered himself and then
a sputtered, "We could have had dinner together. We could
have spent the evening together . . ."

"Uh-huh." I kept my voice carefully neutral.

He switched gears, and his voice suddenly took on that melted caramel tone. "Jess, darlin', I don't know why you're bein' so ornery. I thought I had explained about that scene in the shed. Uh, what you thought you saw, I mean." *What I thought I saw? A spinmeister to the end!*

"Oh, you did explain all that, Shane." The buzzer went off and I struggled to wriggle my right hand into an oven mitt to get the French bread out of the oven. "Uh, Shane, I'm right in the middle of fixing dinner, was there something special you wanted?"

"Well, no, I mean not really," he stammered. Even the Sexiest Teen Alive could sense a blowoff when he got one. "I just called to say I missed you. That's all," he said, with a little edge in his voice. I decided to wait him out. I counted silently to five, and I knew he was steaming. "So, well, I'll see you tomorrow," he said crisply and hung up.

"Was that who I think it was?" Mom asked. "Shane Rockett?"

"The one and only," I said, arranging the bread in a long wicker basket. Funny how just a few days ago, I thought Shane was *my* one and only.

Chapter Fourteen

⭐

THE SKY WAS STILL OVERCAST AND GRAY WHEN I WOKE UP THE next morning. I opened my bedroom window a crack and a gusty wind blew in, ruffling the papers on my desk. I quickly slammed the window shut and stared at the pale sun hidden behind a wall of dark clouds scudding across the sky.

It was lousy weather, but perfect somehow for a day of reckoning. If this really *was* a day of reckoning, I reminded myself. Nothing was definite, after all. Chad Stevens was still in jail, Lu Anne was free, and Crystal was probably still insisting that Gus was the culprit. So much hinged on whether the police could find fingerprints on the camera battery. Was Lu Anne really careless enough to leave them?

I was lost in thought as Tracy and I hurried down Main

Street, putting up the hoods on our windbreakers to ward off a light drizzle that added to the gloom. It was nearly nine o'clock, much later than our usual startup time. They had canceled the usual early-morning call because of the uncertain weather, and I wondered if they would be doing any filming at all.

"What do you think will happen today?" Tracy asked as we slogged across the damp lawn to check the call sheet. I had already eaten breakfast at home but the lemon donuts on the breakfast table were calling to me as we hurried by.

"I don't know," I told her. "Maybe nothing. Things look pretty dead around here." I glanced around the set and saw a few of the cameramen and crew huddled around drinking coffee. Gus was standing talking to a bunch of stuntmen, the extras were herded under a canopy, and Crystal was sitting on a folding chair, a glum expression on her face. There was something eerily still about the scene, but I couldn't put my finger on it.

"Something's wrong," I said softly.

"I know, I feel it too," Tracy said. She was silent for a moment and then snapped her fingers, her eyes flashing. "You know what's missing? Lu Anne."

"Ohmigosh, you're right." No ringing cell phone, no frazzled racing back and forth across the lawn, no ever-present clipboard. No sign of Lu Anne. Where was she? I caught myself wondering if the clipboard would be enough to nail her, just in case the fingerprints didn't show up on the battery. Could they enhance the photo somehow, and prove it was really her clipboard? But what did that really prove? It shows she could have been at the scene, but it didn't prove she was inside the trailer.

"You look like you're pondering the fate of the world," Crystal cackled. "So serious," she said, shaking her head. "When I was your age, I didn't have a thought in my head except what I would wear to the next premiere." She spotted Gus, still talking to the knot of cameramen. "Hah—his days are numbered. I told those nice young detectives my suspicions, and it's just a matter of time," she said smugly. "Just a matter of time," she repeated, staring into her coffee.

Tracy and I exchanged a look. It seemed nothing had happened yet, or Crystal would be spreading the word. "I'm sure things will work out as they're supposed to," I said after a minute. Inwardly, I wasn't so sure. There were too many uncertainties, too many loose ends.

The morning passed quickly and I watched as Sy and Sandy, the assistant director, took some film that would be used later for "establishing shots." Shane and I crossed paths just once as he was coming out of his trailer and I was heading to the production office, but he just nodded and walked away. I smiled, feeling a little glow of accomplishment. Shane's magic hold on me was over. Tracy had noticed the little exchange and grinned as she gave me a thumbs-up.

It was nearly noon when a gaggle of reporters showed up at the south lawn, pushing against the barricade. Tracy and I exchanged a look. If the reporters were here, something must have happened. Was this really the showdown we had hoped for? And where was Lu Anne?

"Look at them," Crystal said acidly. "Vultures, every one of them." She pointed to the reporters who were yelling questions to the crew members setting up a shot at the far edge of the driveway. I couldn't make out the questions, but I thought I heard the word *arrest* a couple of times.

"Just ignore them," Julie cautioned, as she grabbed a cup of coffee. "Sy hired some extra security, but they're not here yet. Don't worry, they'll clear out those reporters in a heartbeat."

"Where's Lu Anne?" I asked, trying to sound casual. "I haven't seen her all morning."

"Oh, she's sick," Julie answered. "She must have picked up some stomach bug last night. Sy said she's spending the whole day in her trailer." She turned to go and then stopped. "Remember, 'no comment,' " she said, "that's all you can say."

"Nice try at damage control," Crystal chortled, "but I don't think it's going to work anymore. Look what's coming up the driveway. I think the game's over, Julie."

I stared in surprise as three police cars, lights on and sirens blaring, roared up the winding entrance to Fairmont. The reporters immediately abandoned their spot at the barricade and switched their attention to the black-and-white police cars. A video photographer moved in for a close shot as Sandy reluctantly moved the barricade aside to let the police on the set.

"What in the world—" Julie began.

"They're finally here to get Gus," Crystal said gleefully. "I knew it would work out in the end!"

A few moments later, the cars screeched to a stop and six uniformed officers surrounded Sy, who had taken off his headset and walked over to greet them. The reporters surged through the open barricade, and the air was filled with the sound of flashbulbs popping and shutters clicking. "Where's Shane? Where's Heidi?" I heard one of the reporters shout. "What do they think about all this? Is it true that Chad Stevens is out of jail?"

A photographer standing next to him trained his camera on me and took a few shots. "What's your name, sweetie?" he shouted. "Are you anybody?"

I ignored him, caught up in the drama in front of me. One of the officers handed Sy a search warrant and Sy nodded and accepted it.

"Why aren't they going after Gus?" Crystal complained. "He's standing right over there." She stood up unsteadily, alarmed at the turn of events. "Look where they're going. They're not even going in the right direction. They're heading to Lu Anne's trailer." She slumped back in her chair with a defeated look on her face. "It just shows you can't trust the cops anymore to know what they're doing."

"I think they know exactly what they're doing," I said quietly.

Shane and Heidi suddenly appeared at the edge of the crowd, looking startled. The reporters lunged forward, popping flashbulbs in their faces before Heidi covered her eyes and scurried back to the safety of her trailer. Shane tried to deflect the photographers, spreading his hands in an expansive gesture, his voice calm.

"Hey, guys, I know you're just doin' your job, but can't you let the cops do their work? You can see there's somethin' serious goin' on here. We'll be glad to talk to you later."

"Give us a break, Shane. We need to talk to you now!"

"We don't need him," another photographer yelled. "Look, they've got somebody in custody." He pointed as the two policemen led Lu Anne out of her trailer in handcuffs. "Who is she?" he muttered.

"She's a nobody," the first reporter muttered. "A real nobody."

Things moved very quickly after that. Lu Anne shot Crystal a defiant look as she was led to the waiting squad car. "It's too bad you didn't fry, you old bag!" she shouted.

Crystal lunged to her feet. "You're the one who set my trailer on fire? What in the world for? I never did anything to you."

Lu Anne blinked back tears, her face red. "Not me, my mother. Rose Carlyle, does that name mean anything to you?"

Crystal looked blank. "Rose Carlyle . . . my God, that was years ago. She was a bit player in one of those spaghetti westerns." She peered closely at Lu Anne. "Rose Carlyle was your mother? Yes, I think I see the resemblance now."

"And you got her fired!" Lu Anne screamed, as the police officer guided her into the backseat of the car. "For nothing! Just because you had the power to do it. You ruined her whole career!"

Crystal paled. "It was all so long ago," she said, shaking her head sadly. "It was all a mistake. She spilled a drink on my dress and I guess I lost my temper. I didn't really want them to fire her." She looked imploringly at me. "Who would think someone would carry a grudge like that?"

When I shook my head and didn't answer, Crystal rested her hand lightly on my arm. "Would you walk me back to my trailer, Jessie? I need to lie down for a while."

"I think the police will want to talk to you," Julie said. The car carrying Lu Anne had sped down the driveway with reporters in hot pursuit, but the other two squad cars remained on the set.

"They can do it later," Sy said, appearing next to us. "Go rest, Crystal, I'll tell the detectives you'll talk to them later. You probably don't have much to tell them, anyway," he said sympathetically. "Who can figure out someone like Lu Anne?

There was a lot more going on there than I realized." He gently put his arm around Crystal. "C'mon, I'll take you back to your trailer myself."

"Nice work, girls." I recognized Detective Aldrich's raspy voice. "Your hunch paid off. She forgot to wipe her prints off the battery. The camera yes, the battery no."

"So she'll be convicted?"

"I don't even think there will be a trial. It's not often you get a public confession like that," he added.

"And not only public, but caught on tape," his partner, Detective Simmons, said. "You heard what she said a minute ago. That's all evidence against her. She'd have a tough time wriggling out of this one. I don't even think she'd try."

"Then it was the picture with the clipboard on the trailer steps that clinched things, after all," I offered. "The one she tried to erase and replace with a new shot."

"Not just the clipboard, but that was a good starting point. There was no reason for her to be in the trailer, unless she was nosing around, looking for a way to cause trouble. And now we know what it was. She must have taken one look at that sofa, and realized it would go up in flames, with a little help. All it would take was a spark from one cigarette. And some flammable liquid."

"She knew Crystal liked to smoke," Tracy said thoughtfully.

"Exactly," Detective Simmons agreed. "She knew Crystal

was bound to light a cigarette in her trailer, so all Lu Anne had to do was sneak back a few days later, sprinkle some flammable fluid on the sofa, and wait for it to happen. One spark would do it. It was only a matter of time."

"And she admitted everything?" I asked.

Detective Simmons nodded. "Lu Anne seemed to realize the game was up. Sometimes people just want to get caught."

Tracy and I locked eyes for a moment. "It's hard to believe it's over," I said softly.

"SO WHAT HAPPENS NEXT?" MOM ASKED LATER THAT DAY. Filming was suspended for the day and I was home for a late lunch. "Will Lu Anne go to jail?"

I shook my head. "Who knows? The whole thing is so sad. Lu Anne thinks that Crystal somehow ruined her mother's acting career and she's been obsessing over it all these years. She thinks that maybe if her mother had been a big star, she would have followed in her footsteps—"

"And so Crystal ruined her dream, too."

"Crazy, isn't it? How one mistake can trail you for the rest of your life." I reached for a loaf of seven-grain bread and smeared a thick slice with apple butter. "At least Chad Stevens is out of jail."

"He never had anything to do with the fire, did he?"

"No, but for some crazy reason, he thought Heidi did it.

And he adores Heidi, almost obsessively. He follows her around like a puppy dog and was willing to take the blame to protect her."

"One thing I've always wondered about," Mom said, pouring herself a glass of mint iced tea, "is that *StarGazer* article. Who really tipped off Rick Morgan?"

"No one knows for sure," I said, "but the word on the set is that Crystal did it. She wanted to get back at Gus. Supposedly he's been blackmailing her over something that happened a long time ago. She wanted to teach him a lesson, maybe even get him fired from the production. When Rick left a phone message, it may have been left in my box by mistake. This is all conjecture, of course." I bit into the crusty bread and leaned back. "And as far as that note telling Tracy to back off, we still don't know who wrote it. It could have been anybody. It could have been Alexis Bright. She was really jealous that Tracy and I were involved with the film, and she was just an extra."

"You didn't know what you were getting into when you took the part, did you? I think this movie has been a learning experience for you," my mother said softly.

"In more ways than one." My mind drifted back to Shane and Heidi: I thought I had found the love of my life and a new best friend. And they both had vanished . . .

"What's going to happen with *Reckless Summer*?"

"Sy said we're going to wrap up filming here in another

three days. Then they're going to head back to California and shoot the rest of it there. There's too much publicity in Bedford to deal with. He said he'd be hounded by reporters night and day if he stayed."

"Are you disappointed?" She looked searchingly at me over the rim of her glass.

"No, I'm fine with it. Honest," I added, when I saw a flicker of doubt cross her face. "I'm kind of glad my part in it is over. Maybe I can find something else to do with the rest of my summer."

"Oh, I'm sure you can," Mom said, looking mysterious. "By the way, did you check the message board when you came in?" She pointed to the antique slate we keep propped at the edge of the kitchen desk. Her eyes were twinkling in a way that made me think something special was on there, so I decided to be supercool about it.

"Not yet, I thought I'd do it after lunch," I said, playing the game.

"Okay," she said, getting up to refill her tea. "But I'd do it sooner rather than later. I think you might have an interesting summer after all."

"You do?" Now I was dying to check the board, but I wanted to see how long I could hold out. "Why's that?"

"Well, a certain young man from New Orleans—a handsome young man, I might add—just happened to call, and said they were offering a special fare to his city. He and his parents were wondering if you would like to pay them a visit? Naturally, I told him you were busy with filming—"

"You told him what?" I squealed.

"Relax, I'm just kidding," she said with a throaty chuckle. "I told him I thought there was a very good possibility you'd be free to fly down there . . ."

I raced to the message board and saw Marc's number scrawled there. I grinned at Mom. "I'll call him later tonight when the rates go down . . ."

She flashed me a big smile. "Oh, I think this calls for a celebration. Why don't you strike while the iron is hot and call him now? On me," she said, tossing me her cell phone.

My heart was skittering in my chest as I dialed Marc's number. I think I forgot to breathe as it rang four times before he picked it up. "The Black Swan," he said crisply. I heard dishes clattering in the background and I realized they were probably in the middle of serving lunch. I imagined the wrought-iron umbrella tables, the sweet scent of magnolia in the air, and Marc's sexy smile as he greeted the customers. I suddenly had an unbearable urge to be with him, to hold him, to kiss him.

"Hi Marc," I said, feeling a little shy, "it's me."

"Oh *cher*, I hoped you would call." His voice was like a caress, rippling over my skin, setting my nerve endings tingling. "I've missed you so much. I have so much to tell you . . ."

"Well, you can tell me in person," I said laughingly.

"Because I'm going to take you up on that invitation to fly down to New Orleans. Tell your mom I can be there by next weekend."

"By next weekend? That's exactly what I've been hoping for! There's a big celebration in the Vieux Carre on Saturday night, Jessie. Fireworks and rock bands, big-name performers. We can watch it all from Bourbon Street."

Bourbon Street. I flashed on a romantic dinner the two of us had last summer at a little outdoor café in the French Quarter. We had held hands and barely touched our dinners, while a guitar player hovered near the table playing love songs. "It sounds terrific."

"Oh, it will be. Just think, we can spend the whole summer together. Just the two of us. You won't believe the plans I have for us . . ."

I listened to his deep voice crackling over the line, my heart doing a double tap dance in my chest, and suddenly I knew everything was going to be all right. Nothing was ruined. I hadn't blown my chances with Marc, and we would see each other soon in New Orleans. Very soon.

Because sometimes things have a way of working out after all.

books

COMING THIS SUMMER
A TOTALLY FRESH LINE OF BOOKS

<u>May 2005</u>
SO LYRICAL
by Trish Cook
0-451-21508-7

<u>June 2005</u>
ROCK MY WORLD
by Lisa Conrad
0-451-21523-0

<u>July 2005</u>
THE PRINCIPLES OF LOVE
by Emily Franklin
0-451-21517-6

CONFESSIONS OF AN ALMOST–MOVIE STAR
by Mary Kennedy
0-425-20467-7

<u>August 2005</u>
JENNIFER SCALES AND THE ANCIENT FURNACE
by MaryJanice Davidson
and Anthony Alongi
0-425-20598-3

Available in paperback from Berkley and New American Library

www.penguin.com